Leo Kessler is a familiar name to readers of war fiction. In addition to his numerous super-selling war series, he is the author of several non-fiction works and of the screenplay *Breakthrough*. He lives in Germany between energetic bouts of travelling.

D0801174

Also by Leo Kessler

Leo Kessler

Otto Stahl 3
Otto and the Reds

Futura
Macdonald & Co
London & Sydney

A Futura Book

First published in Great Britain in 1982
by Futura Publications, a Division of Macdonald & Co
(Publishers) Ltd
London & Sydney

ISBN 0 7088 2196 0

Filmset, printed and bound in Great Britain by
Hazell Watson & Viney Ltd, Aylesbury, Bucks

Futura Publications
A Division of
Macdonald & Co (Publishers) Ltd
Maxwell House
74 Worship Street
London EC2A 2EN

OTTO AND THE REDS

RUSSIA, *1941–1942*

'He who eats with the Devil needs a long spoon.'
Old German Saying

L.K.

A few words from Señor OTTO M. STAHL

That scribbler guy Kessler has asked me to write this. I know why. You don't need to be a crapping genius to figure out that he and that fancy-pants, old-Etonian publisher of his over there in London are *ashamed* of me. They want me to show myself up by writing this, to let you know what kind of slob I am, or so they think, the shitehawks.

You see, I'm not a hero like those other dum-dums Kessler writes about. Of course, I've had enough shit flung at me in three wars – but I never pretended to be a hero. That's why *I'm* here nearly forty years later, and all Kessler's so-called 'heroes' are long dead in some crummy, God-forsaken corner of the Soviet workers' paradise that's probably not even marked on the map.

I'm common, too. I know they think that behind my back. Just because I don't drink my coffee with my little pinky stuck out at an angle like some goddam fairy-queen, and I like to let a good old fart rip once in a while. Who could blame me with the kind of grub these Spanish dagos serve?

Kessler and that old-Etonian friend of his don't exactly shit through the ribs either, as we used to say in the old days. And what's more, they don't exactly blush with shame when they charge off to the bank with the dough I've earned them with my story. *No, sir!* As for the rest of you, well, you're getting a good tale, a damned good tale – *real class*, if I do say so myself. So what *you* think about Mrs Stahl's handsome son don't worry me one little bit.

In my time I've gone off a lot of people. I don't like the

Dutch cheeseheads. I don't like frogs. I don't like the paddies – what dum-dums *they* are! Perhaps it's a good thing they're knocking each other's brains out again! I don't like the spaghetti-eaters. I don't like the Krauts. I don't like . . . Well, I could go off the Tommies right smartish as well, if I felt like it. It's only money I get for this, after all. I don't expect the Queen to invite me to Buck Palace for a cup of nigger sweat and crumpets and pin a putty medal on my chest for services to literature, you know. Besides, I've got a drawerful of fancy-coloured tin upstairs as it is. Medals, I've shat them!

So, what am I trying to say? This. I've let Kessler write up my experiences in Russia in 1941, just after Adolf launched his great 'crusade' against the Bolshies. Jesus H. Christ, some crusade! It's a war book. The real McCoy. It's not about your high-ranking, creamcake-arses of rear echelon stallions, having it off with classy countesses in fancy frilly knickers in some big chateau, kilometres behind the front. Nor about your four-eyed bleeding-heart, parlour-pink intellectuals running off at the mouth about the 'horrors of war'. No, sir! This is the way it really was. What did your good old Churchill say? (By the way, a good guy for my book. You could use a half-dozen of his kind over there in England these days to heave your hooters out of the crap.) 'Blood, sweat and tears'? Well, this book is all '*shit, shot and shell!*' Because, believe you me, war ain't pretty. Not a bit like the way those fairies show it on the tube. No way!

Sometimes, me and Kessler have thought of putting the odd booby-trap in a couple of these books of mine; or perhaps a nice lethal little anti-personnel mine – to kill or maim a few readers. That'd teach you lot what war was *really* like. But don't worry, folks. It's against the law to kill yer readers. Besides, it's bad for business – and with the cost of living here on the coast going through the roof, I need the dough.

So, I've said my piece. Piss or get off the pot, as they

used to say in the old days. Now you know that Mrs Stahl's handsome son is no hero, that he's common, that he takes no shit from anybody and that he couldn't care a monkey's what you lot think of him. O.K. – now you can get on with it! Read it! And don't worry, when you read it: you'll survive . . .

Otto M. Stahl, Denia, Spain, December 1980.

BOOK ONE: BARBAROSSA

'When Barbarossa commences, the world will hold its breath.'

Adolf Hitler, 1941

ONE

'*Los Braun!*' the tremendous, hoarse voice thundered across the still hot Rumanian air.

'*Come on, you arse with plush ears! Get stuck in! And you, Hinze, on the left flank – put some pepper in yer pants, or by the Great Jehovah and all his Yiddish triangles, I'll have the knickers off 'n yer and award yer the Order of the Purple Shaft before this day is out . . .*'

Otto Stahl groaned. Everybody in the Adolf Hitler Bodyguard seemed to shout all the time, but nobody as much as Hairless Horst Hartung, the 1st Battalion's Sergeant-Major. Cautiously he raised his naked body by the elbows and peered out of the window.

Across the drill square, a burning dusty white in the hot June sunshine, little figures, their uniforms black with sweat, were racing, bayonets fixed, towards a wooden bunker, firing blanks as they ran; others, strange round packs on their shoulders, were approaching it from the flank more cautiously.

Curiosity got the better of the handsome young man. Momentarily he forgot Gerda and her importunings, splendid and expert as they were, and watched the mock attack below. Stroking the mass of golden curls draped across his lean stomach in absent-minded encouragement, he observed as the grenadiers flung themselves down in the dust some fifty metres from the wooden bunker and started to rattle off blank ammunition at it, while the men with the strange packs crept through the dead ground towards the same objective.

At his loins Gerda was working herself up into a frenzy.

He patted her head again encouragingly. She was doing very well for such a very hot day.

'*Now!*' screeched Hairless Horst.

The men with the packs came to a ragged halt. Hoses appeared in their hands as they stood there, legs apart, gasping furiously, waiting for the gigantic NCO's next command.

'*Fire!*' he cried.

Everywhere the window panes rattled.

There was a sudden hush as if some primeval fire-breathing monster were drawing a breath. With dramatic suddenness, tongues of evil dark-blue flames tinged with oily smoke shot out of the hose, wreathing the wooden bunker with fervent fury. With a dry crackle, the wood ignited and the air was suddenly filled with the acrid stink of burning wood and sandbags.

'You've done it!' Hairless Horst cried in delight. 'You've done it, you bunch of perverted banana-suckers!' He ripped off his too-small helmet to reveal a perfectly bald head. '*Done it in five minutes, flat!*' He threw his helmet to the ground enthusiastically.

'I've done it, Otto!' Gerda, Horst's wife, said proudly, raising her head for the first time since they had got into bed together for their customary after-lunch session.

Otto forgot the strange little exercise outside. He looked down and said, almost as if surprised, 'So you have.'

She beamed up at him, her pretty face flushed crimson and damp with sweat at the exertion.

'The beast with two backs?' he suggested.

'Oh, please, Otto darling,' she squeaked excitedly.

He reached for her plump, proud breasts with his big, expert hands. 'All right then, roll over, Gerda. The beast with two backs it will be . . .'

'These days,' the red-faced, exhausted young grenadier was telling his companion, 'they'll take anybody in the

Bodyguard. Not like before the war – we were an élite then. Why, some hairy-arsed stubble-hopper with no arms went up for his medical the other day and still the bone-menders took him. So when he gets up here to the Bodyguard, old General Dietrich says to him, "You got no arms, son? No matter. There's always a place for a keen type like you in the Bodyguard. Just go across and help those two cardboard soldiers over there pumping water into buckets." "But I can't help them, General," the arse without arms says. "I ain't got no flippers." "Don't worry," old Sepp Dietrich says. "You just tell them when to stop – *they're both blind!*" '

His companion laughed hollowly, as did Otto. He had heard the hoary old tale before, too. Now it was four o'clock on this burningly hot day and, as both men could see, the Bodyguard were still hard at their training; it looked as if time were running out and the premier division of the Armed SS were desperate to pack in all the marches and exercises they could before it was too late.

Otto took his gaze off Gerda's husband, Hairless Horst. It wasn't hard. The big NCO had the ugly face and close-set eyes of a man who had been sold short on brains but who had been liberally endowed with muscles by way of compensation. He took a sip of his chilled *tokay* and said lazily, 'What do you make of it, Count?'

Count von der Weide, Otto's running-mate of these last three years of war, spat out a mouthful of sunflower seeds, which, together with the balalaika he had taken up the week before and his collarless Russian peasant blouse, went to make up his new Russian identity. 'Make of what, little brother?' he asked in oddly-accented German.

'Oh, come off it, Count,' Otto said. 'I mean Hairless Horst chasing those lads of his all over the place like that, and all the coming and going at Dietrich's HQ.'

'That?' The Count rolled his eyes. 'War, of course.'

Otto slapped his forehead in mock rage. The middle-aged Count had recruited him into the German Secret

Service from Aachen Jail three years ago, and Otto liked him well enough; but his moods and his habit of self-dramatization took some getting used to.[1] 'Count, it may have escaped your notice perhaps, but we have had a war since 1939. What war do you shitting well mean? That little boy-scout game the buck-teethed Tommies in their long khaki drawers are playing with Rommel in the Western Desert, eh?'

'No, not that, Otto.' The Count strummed a chord on his triangular-shaped instrument. 'I mean war out there.' He gestured towards the burning horizon where the sun glowed copper-coloured behind the heat haze like a coin glimpsed at the bottom of a green-scummed pond. 'There in Mother Russia.'

'Russia?' Otto echoed, appalled. 'But the Russians are supposed to be our allies. We've had a pact with Stalin since 1939. We're not going to let them attack us, are we?'

The Count shook his head. 'Otto, my dear boy, the Führer is the one who will do the attacking, and—' he hesitated a fraction of a second, as if he did not quite know whether he should express his thoughts '—I am afraid that General Dietrich has found some sort of a role for us in *that* attack.'

'What!' Otto began aghast. But before he could continue with his question the sticky bomb which Hairless Horst had just been demonstrating to a group of the new recruits to the Bodyguard to make up for their losses in Greece exploded in the hands of one of the unfortunate young men and a head came rolling Otto's way, complete with helmet, to trail to a bloody stop at his feet like an abandoned football.

Down below, Hairless Horst put his ham-like fists on his hips, legs spread well apart, and quaked with laughter at the look on Otto's face as he stared down at the severed head lying at his feet. 'Shook you civvies up a bit, eh?' he cried, tears of mirth streaming down his crimson, stupid

[1] See *Otto's Phoney War* for further details.

face. 'Shook him up a bit, too, I shouldn't wonder.' He pointed to the smoking remains of the dead youth. 'Always said to General Dietrich that those sticky bombs were dangerous. Tend to stick to your flippers if you're not careful. All right, first three numbers in the front row, off at the double and get shovels and pails. Don't want the place to look a mess, now do we? Now, as I was saying, the sticky bomb weighs four kilos and . . .'

'*Arse!*' Otto said thickly, trying to restrain himself from being sick.

'Soldiers – salt of the earth,' the Count murmured somewhat vaguely and strummed his balalaika again. Meanwhile the head stared up at the two of them accusingly, as if to say, 'Well, come on, don't mess about – *pick me up!*'

Just at that moment, Baltz, General Dietz's personal orderly, snapped to attention before them and saluted as if they were very important people indeed. '*Der Herr General lässt bitten.*'

The Count stopped his playing. 'The conference?' he asked almost eagerly, as if he had been waiting a long time for this invitation to Standartenführer Dietrich's HQ.

'Yes, Count,' Baltz barked.

'When?'

'Tonight, after dinner, sir. All the officers are invited.'

The Count looked at Otto. 'This is it, my boy. It will make history!'

Otto groaned and stepped carefully over the severed head. 'I don't like history, Count,' he said. 'It stinks – and besides, people die in history. People like us in particular,' he added darkly, as he started to trail back to their quarters. After a moment the Count followed, strumming his balalaika and humming a Russian folk song to himself, a happy smile on his fleshy, handsome face.

TWO

Standartenführer Sepp Dietrich was obviously in high good humour. He was surrounded by his slim, elegant young officers, all a good head taller than he and was dipping the end of his cigar in his glass of cognac and puffing at it.

'Doors secured, sentries posted,' Hairless Horst barked from the door. 'Room hermetically sealed now, Standartenführer!'

Dietrich waved for him to go and then impatiently waited while the big NCO locked the door to the conference room behind him. Then he strode to the wall and drew a pair of curtains with a flourish to reveal a large map. 'Russia, comrades! The workers' paradise!' The words were spat out with a thick Bavarian accent.

There was a gasp from his officers, even though they had been expecting this announcement for several days now. 'We attack, Standartenführer?' Major Fray, the tallest of the Bodyguard's officers, asked eagerly.

'We attack. At four-thirty exactly on the morning of June 22nd, 1941. Operation Barbarossa, the Führer has named the operation.' His broad peasant face grew hard. 'When Barbarossa commences, the Führer has said, "the world will hold its breath!" '

Otto, standing at the edge of the crowd of officers, flashed the Count a significant look but immediately saw that the latter was completely absorbed with Dietrich's announcement.

Otto shook his head. The Count was just as naive and gullible as these soldiers half his age. He would never grow up if he lived to be a hundred. Suddenly an alarming thought occurred to the handsome young man with the deep blue eyes. Perhaps, if what he suspected was going to happen *did* happen, neither of them would ever reach half that age.

'The infantry of the Von Manstein Army Group to which the Bodyguard will belong when the balloon goes up, comrades,' Dietrich continued, 'will have the initial task of forcing the Russians' first lines of defences *here, here* and *here!*' He jabbed the big map with his cigar while his officers craned their necks to note the points. 'The actual date of our own employment will depend just how long it takes the stubble-hoppers from the Army to make the breakthrough. But whenever it is, comrades,' Dietrich's voice rose, 'we will chase those Ivan arses as if they were the lily-white bottoms of delicately brought-up daughters of elderly clergymen!'

There was a burst of laughter at the stocky General's crudity. Dietrich could never conceal the fact that he had been a cavalry sergeant in the First War. But the General himself appeared not to hear the laughter. He continued, his voice hard and urgent: 'There must be no let-up, whatever the casualties. We must keep striking and striking them until they are on their knees and then strike them again!' In his urgency he crushed the cigar to pulp in his big hand without even noticing it. 'The Führer has given us the very special honour of leading the break-out and we must not let him down. After all, we bear his own name.'

There was a murmur of agreement from the young officers, and Dietrich seemed to calm down a little. 'Of course, there will be decorations for you all, if you succeed. By the time Barbarossa is over, you will have drawerfuls of the things, undoubtedly those of you who survive will be boring your grandchildren with the details of how you won your scrambled egg and cured your throat-ache fifty years from now.'

Again his officers laughed. A worried Otto looking at

their eager young faces, wreathed with smiles now, wondered just how many of them would ever have grandchildren – or even children, for that matter. Somehow he
rather doubted that the attack on Russia would be the kind
of walk-over that the campaigns in the West and the
Balkans had been. The Russians were a tough people;
they'd fight back all right. He was sure of that.

'Now to details, comrades,' Dietrich went on. With the
aid of the map he started to rap out objectives and aims for
the various battalions under his command, while their
respective commanders made notes on their own maps or
scribbled down pieces of information in their pads. Otto,
meanwhile, wondered just how he would cope with the
insatiable Gerda once old Hairless Horst, her prick of a
husband, was sent to the front. My God – he'd be at her
mercy twenty-four hours a day!

Then the briefing was over and the officers were streaming out chattering excitedly among themselves, hurrying
off to their own various headquarters to start working out
individual battalion plans. Otto breathed a sigh of relief.
So they'd managed to get away with it: they weren't going
to be needed after all – in spite of the fact that they had
been let into the secret of the new war.

Hastily he grabbed the Count's arm. 'Come on, Count.
Let's not waste the good General's time—'

The words died on his lips. Dietrich was beaming at
them, giving the two civilians the full benefit of his
splendid array of gold teeth. Otto's heart sank. The shit,
he realized, was about to hit the fan with great vigour . . .

Dietrich sat opposite them, bottle of beer in one hand,
glass of Schnapps in the other, tunic ripped open. Now
that his officers had departed he could once again be the
simple-minded, coarse-mouthed noncom that he had
always remained at heart, in spite of his general's rank.

'Soldiers are a simple lot,' he said, a little thickly; he had already drunk quite a deal at dinner. 'The way you tell 'em things has got to be simple too, so that you don't confuse them.' His dark eyes sparkled.

'You have the soul of a Russian,' the Count said obscurely.

'And the arse of one, too,' Dietrich said. 'Now I didn't want to worry my officers, but there's just one little problem after the initial breakthrough which we must overcome if we're going to keep within the time-limits set for the Bodyguard by that aristocratic ape-shit von Manstein.'

'It is, General?' the Count asked.

'The Miropol Position, some fifty kilometres from our start-line. You see, Count, we have next to nothing in the way of information about the Soviet workers' paradise. In the last sixteen months or so we've captured the military archives of Holland, Belgium, Greece, Jugoslavia and even those of the Frog General Staff. But to my way of thinking none of those countries was any better informed about the Russians than we are. I mean, even the maps we got from them have turned out to be wrong, according to aerial recon. The roads they marked nice, thick and red on their maps turn out to be tracks. Tracks turn out to be first-class roads – it's absolutely bloody hopeless.' He took a pull at his Schnapps, grimaced, as if he wished he hadn't, and hastily guzzled down some beer to take away the taste.

The Count beamed at him. 'We've got the job?' he asked quickly.

Dietrich belched and nodded.

The Count looked delighted. 'Just our collar-size!' he exclaimed. 'What an adventure it will be. If—'

'—Gentlemen, *please*,' Otto broke in. 'What job is this? Please tell me, would you. I'm only a simple working-class boy from Berlin-Wedding. You'll have to explain things nice and slow and simple to me so that my ignorant working-class brain can take it in.'

'It's the Miropol Position,' Dietrich said. 'As I said, we

know so little of the Ivan dispositions. There's a rumour that the place is a second kind of *Westwall*,[1] but recon. photos show us little. So, if I don't want my sardine cans running straight into some fortified line, I've got to know the actual strength of the place – *now!*'

Otto recalled Hairless Horst chasing his men against the wooden bunker that afternoon and the attack from the flank with the flame-throwers. So that was what that little exercise had been about. 'You said *now*, Standartenführer?' he asked carefully, already half-knowing what Dietrich's answer to his final question would be. 'How can information about those positions be obtained *now* . . . please?'

'Well, Herr Stahl, your reputation is well known to me. You're not like those other aristocratic warm brothers of Intelligence – excuse my French, Count, but you understand what I mean? It's known widely that most of those Intelligence fellows wear frilly laced knickers and party frocks on Saturday nights. But you two are different, you are men of action—'

'—*Now?*' Otto interrupted Dietrich's flow of words.

'Well,' Dietrich said, 'Fat Hermann—' referring to the head of the Luftwaffe, Hermann Goering '—has lent me a plane and a pilot for two days.' He looked significantly at a suddenly pale-faced Otto.

'And you want me and the Count here to land behind the Soviet frontier, find out as much as we can about this – er – Miropol Position and then return by the same means?'

'Exactly. If any agents can pull it off, you can. We land you about five kilometres from your objective – at night, of course.'

'Of course!' the Count echoed enthusiastically.

'Give you the day to find out what type of armament and that sort of thing the Popovs have over there, then you lie up until the plane picks you up again. A simple two-day job.'

[1] The Siegfried Line.

'But we don't speak Russian, and we have no papers,' Otto protested.

'*Boshe moi*,' the Count snapped in Russian and struck his chest. 'The time for words is over. Action at last! How grateful we are to you, my dear General, for this opportunity to participate in the great crusade against the Bolshevik beast, are we not, Otto, my dear boy?'

'When?' was all that Otto could say.

'Tonight at midnight,' General Dietrich answered, obviously confident now that everything had been taken care of and that from here onwards everything would simply be glory, glory all the way.

Otto farted with fear.

THREE

'Pistols,' Hairless Horst said, 'Italian berettas – sign here.'

Duly the two men signed. Outside, there was no sound now save that of tired snores from the open windows of the Rumanian barracks and the soft tread of the sentries as they paced their beats on the gravelled walks.

'Five hundred rubles each,' Hairless Horst continued, 'sign here.'

'What do we need rubles for?' Otto objected. 'We're not going to be around long enough for shopping expeditions.'

Hairless Horst shrugged. 'Don't ask me, civvie. Duty's duty and Schnapps is Schnapps. I'm just doing what I've been told to be doing by the Chief Intelligence Officer. L-Pill.'

'L-Pill?' both Otto and the Count asked in unison, staring down at the last item of kit on the table in front of them, a tiny capsule gleaming a dull white in the flickering light thrown by the hissing petroleum lamp.

'L for Lethal,' the big Sergeant-Major answered. 'Screw it into the back of yer wisdom tooth, in case the Popovs catch yer.' He sniffed and looked hard at Otto. For a moment the latter wondered whether the giant NCO knew just how generous his wife Gerda had been with her favours of late. 'If they do, you're to swallow it toot-sweet, as the frogs say. The Intelligence Officer was very strict about that. Can't give anything away about the new mission.'

'How good of him to be so concerned about our welfare,' Otto commented sourly, tucking the pill in the breast-pocket of his shirt. He was supposed to be wearing a Russian farmer's blouse – it smelt like the real thing at least: a combination of black tobacco, garlic, sweat and horse-shit.

The Count followed suit, remarking, 'You don't seem to be very happy tonight, my dear Sergeant-Major. I thought the prospect of the great adventure before us might have induced a good mood.'

'Don't mind a bit of murder and mayhem, Herr Graf. I mean, that's what a soldier gets paid for – to knock people's heads in. But it's my Gerda,' he added a little miserably.

'Your Gerda?' Otto asked cautiously.

'Now we're going to have a bit of trouble with the Popovs, we senior noncoms have got to send our wives back to the Reich.' He sniffed. 'God only knows how my Gerda is going to make out all alone in Berlin without me – she's so shy! A proper little innocent wallflower, if I say so myself.'

Otto said nothing as they started out into the warm night toward the waiting car; but he wondered what the big NCO would have said if he had seen his poor innocent Gerda out in the back of the officers' mess only two hours ago. Holy strawsack – she had almost ripped off his fly-buttons in her eagerness to get at it! For a brief, frightening moment he had been worried about his manhood! By the time the big fool of an NCO came back from the attack on Russia – if he ever *did* come back – his Gerda would have had the pants off the entire male population of Berlin, including the choirboys in the Kaiser Wilhelm Memorial Church.

Otto clambered into the back seat of the Opel Wanderer, and the Count followed him, while the big NCO squeezed behind the wheel and started the motor. 'You're strangely silent, Otto,' the Count said.

'Don't talk to me, Count,' Otto grunted. 'I'm in no mood for chat.'

'Problems?'

'Yes, suicidal ones. Now shut up, please!'

The two civilians sank back in the seat, as the car moved

off into the darkness, its little blue beams feeling the way through the blackout.

Otto sank into gloomy contemplation, trying to penetrate the sombre shadows of that endless, ghost-ridden Rumanian plain which ran right to the frontier with Russia. What lay ahead for them out there? he wondered. Why was it that, after three years of trying to avoid the war, not merely because he was something of a coward, but also because he didn't want to fight for Hitler and all he stood for, he and the Count always ended up taking part in some impossible adventure? It had been the same in Belgium, then Holland, then later in 1940 and 1941 in England and Greece.[1] Was it the Count's fault, with his impossible flamboyant style and lack of contact with reality? Or was it his own? Was he not after all a German, who couldn't divorce his own fate from that of his people, in spite of his hatred of National Socialism? Or was he, the smart, knowing son of a working-class Berlin whoremother and professional pavement-pounder, simply one of nature's fools? A lot of questions and very few answers . . .

Otto's thoughts tailed off into nothing. Beside him, as the dark Rumanian countryside rolled by, and the air became filled with the heavy scent of pine resin, the Count strummed on his balalaika plaintively, as if he, too, for once was actually considering the seriousness of their situation. Otto Stahl and Graf von der Weide were going out into the unknown once more. Anything could happen.

Hairless Horst braked sharply next to a large, strangely shaped stone, clearly outlined now in the moonlight. Otto woke from his doze with a start.

Next to him the Count said, 'We're here. That's the phallic symbol General Dietrich told me about. Quite impressive, isn't it? It must be at least ten metres high.'

'I was the model, Count,' Hairless Horst grunted with

[1] See *Otto's Phoney War* and *Otto's Blitzkrieg*.

a grimace. 'Don't make 'em like me any more. When *I've* had 'em, they stay had!' He thrust out his barrel chest proudly.

'Why don't you stick it up your arse and give yourself a cheap thrill, then?' Otto said sourly and clambered out of the car. He could now see the dark outline of the Fieseler Storch some fifty metres away, with the mechanics already busy around it, preparing the monoplane for the flight across the Russian border.

'Our tame civvie getting a bit nervous, eh?' Hairless Horst said without rancour. 'Better keep yer legs crossed and yer arsehole tight for the next sixty minutes or there might be an unpleasant accident, Stahl.'

Before Otto could find a suitable riposte, a tall figure staggered out of the darkness and said, slurring his words badly, 'Ah, the gentlemen from the Abwehr, what?'

Hairless Horst swung up his torch and by its blue beam, Otto saw a good-natured drinker's face set above the Knight's Cross of the Iron Cross which rested in what appeared to be a pair of frilly ladies' knickers. Hastily he clicked to attention and boomed, 'One NCO, two civvies, all present and correct, Herr Oberleutnant!'

The pilot gave a mock groan and clapped his hand to his head, as if it had suddenly begun to ache severely. 'Holy Strawsack, Sergeant-Major, must you bellow so? You'll wake every Popov from here to Moscow. Keep it down to a dull roar, there's a good chap, what.'

'Sorry, sir,' Horst said and then turned to Otto and the Count, fumbling with his notebook. 'Sign here that I've delivered you safe and sound,' he demanded. 'General's orders.'

Grumbling a little, they did so, while the pilot leaned against the side of the Opel Wanderer and took a sip of some sort of alcohol from a silver flask.

Once more Hairless Horst clicked to attention and then, happy to have 'delivered his bodies' safely, he swung behind the wheel and started the motor once more, as if he were now in a hurry to get back to his poor innocent Gerda.

'Hope I've given her the crabs,' Otto said sourly, as the car moved off. 'Then you'll have something to remember me by.'

Five minutes later the mechanics had equipped them with thick, fur-lined coveralls and were busy strapping them into cumbersome parachutes and heavy leather flying-helmets, while the pilot briefed them on what was to come, all the time taking sips from his silver flask. 'Flight time thirty minutes at the most. Got a good tail-wind, so I should be able to set you down right on time in a little copse I've picked out, nice and secluded. The old Storch can touch down anywhere,' he said confidently, '—on the left labia of an undersized Chink virgin, if you like.' He roared with laughter at his own attempt at humour, while Otto looked severely at the Count. Were pilots supposed to drink when they were on operations? the look read.

The Count shrugged uneasily, for now the ground crew, almost finished with their tasks, were also pulling out bottles of beer and potent Rumanian plum brandy, and taking deep, grateful swigs of the liquid.

'We don't know a thing about their flak, but not to worry, chaps. I'll fly the old crate at ground level so they'll never even see us. Anyway, you'll be off and on your mission within the hour. Tomorrow night I'll pick you up at the same time and same spot *exactly*. Got it down to a fine art, haven't I, chaps?'

'*Jawohl, Herr Oberleutnant*,' the happy ground crew chortled in unison. One of them fell over as he fumbled under the aircraft for another bottle and immediately began to snore softly.

'If you've got it down to a fine art,' Otto asked, 'why have we been fitted out with these shitting silk umbrellas?' He touched his parachute. 'I don't fancy the idea of taking little walks across the night sky.'

'Simply routine, old chap,' the pilot said airily. 'Orders

from above, you know. Can't have civvies wandering around without a chute. S.O.P.'

'S.O.P.?' the Count queried.

'Standard Operating Procedure.'

'I suppose you've done this sort of thing many times before?' the Count asked hopefully as the pilot reached over and took a bottle of plum brandy from one of the mechanics.

'Very first time, as a matter of fact,' the pilot answered. 'Used to be in fighters. Said I smashed up too many crates.' He shrugged and took a deep swig of the red liquid. 'Now I'm with this lot.' He started to stagger towards the cockpit, rattling off orders as he went.

'I knew it,' Otto said, as they waddled after him in their heavy gear. 'I shitting well knew it.'

The Count smiled. 'As the English writer Stevenson said once, my boy, "our business in life is not to succeed, but to continue to fail in good spirits".'

'I can't find the arse-holing chocks,' was the last thing Otto heard, uttered in a drunken voice from the ground, as the Fieseler's motors burst into violent life and the little monoplane began to vibrate alarmingly. 'Can't find 'em anywhere, Herr Oberleutnant!'

Groaning miserably, Otto abandoned himself to his fate . . .

Shortly after they crossed the border there came a strange rapping noise from down below, like the beak of some gigantic raven tapping against an egg and trying to free its imprisoned brood.

'I say,' the Oberleutnant's voice came crackling metallicly over the intercom, 'I wonder what—'

His sentence remained unfinished.

Next moment the plane swung violently to port and as Otto grabbed for his throat to prevent himself from vomiting there and then, there was a tremendous violet flash to their front.

The Count blinked his eyes rapidly, trying to recover his sight. 'In three devils' name, what *is* that?' he croaked.

'I can tell you, you silly shit!' Otto cried, as everywhere searchlights flicked on and began to part the night sky with their silver-ice fingers, '*The Popovs are firing at us!*'

'Great crap on the Christmas Tree!' the pilot exclaimed. Since take-off he had been flying with one hand on the controls and the other wrapped protectively round his silver flask. Now for the first time he let go of it. 'I think you could be right.'

'Of course I'm right—' Otto's words were drowned by another burst of shell fire. Silver-grey cotton puffballs of smoke were exploding on both sides of the little plane, buffeting it from left to right, as if in the grip of some enormous tornado.

'Keep your hair on!' the pilot cried. 'I've seen worse things at sea!' he added jauntily. 'I'll soon clear those asparagus Tarzans off the trees.'

As the first searchlight flooded the cabin, illuminating the two civilians' faces in stark, glowing fear, the pilot, face set and determined, throttled back abruptly. The cabin darkened at once as the plane slipped out of the beam. '*Hold on to your eggs, gents!*' the pilot screamed, exhilarated by the sudden action, and started to drop.

Otto's stomach seemed to go through the roof of his mouth. Next to him the Count pulled off his intercom; obviously he was being violently sick.

One hundred metres . . . one hundred and fifty metres . . . They continued to drop at a tremendous, stomach-churning rate. Above them the shells exploded harmlessly in bright gasps of flame . . . two hundred metres . . . two hundred and fifty metres . . .

Just when Otto thought they were going to hit the ground, the pilot, shouting crazily to himself, revved the engine. The little monoplane picked up immediately, while the guns continued to hammer and the angry searchlights flashed back and forth across the velvet expanse of the night sky, looking in vain for their elusive prey.

Otto breathed out a sigh of relief and croaked weakly, 'Hope you don't do that too often, Herr Oberleutnant – there's something wet and warm trickling down my left leg already.'

Next to him, the Count added faintly, 'Do you think it would be possible for me to get out at the next stop? I'm afraid I've had a little accident.'

'Nothing to worry about, chaps,' the pilot said heartily, as if this was all in a day's work. 'Bit off course, I think. But my guess is that we'll be over the landing strip in a couple of minutes or more. Soon have you down in old Mother Russia, getting on with the old cloak-and-dagger stuff.'

'Anything,' the Count said weakly, 'but just get us down.'

'I will . . . I will.'

But it was not to be.

They were flying at perhaps three hundred metres, with the pilot searching for the landing spot which he claimed lay somewhere to port, quite close to a small, hilly, wooded area – when it happened. There was a series of soft pops, and suddenly what looked like golden ping-pong balls were curving up towards the plane from starboard, at first slowly and then gathering speed at a tremendous rate.

'*Achtung!*' Otto cried, reacting quicker than the pilot, who was still concentrating on the landing. 'Tracer from the—'

Too late!

A shower of lead smacked into the length of the fuselage like heavy tropical raindrops on a tin roof and the cabin was suddenly filled with the acrid stench of cordite. The perspex of the cockpit shattered into a crazy, gleaming spider's web.

'*Scheisse!*' the pilot screamed, shrill and hysterical, as the slugs ripped his arm open and the blood started to jet out of a severed artery in a scarlet fountain. Already the Fieseler's engine was beginning to cough and splutter alarmingly, and Otto could see that the Oberleutnant was not going to survive much longer: as he attempted to regain control, his hands seemed as slow and as thick as if they were packed in heavyweight boxing gloves.

The plane gave another lurch. Yet another salvo of slugs ripped the length of the fabric, and now the two deathly-scared civilians could feel the blast of cold air coming in on all sides. The pilot started to slump over his controls. The Fieseler's nose tilted. The coughing and spluttering of the plane's engine grew ever more acute. Instinctively, Otto knew that the plane's end was near; there was no hope of the pilot ever rescuing her now. He ripped the intercom from his helmet and indicated the Count should do the same.

The engine died. Now there was no sound save the hiss of the wind in the struts and the harsh, rapid breathing of the dying pilot.

Fighting his way through the shattered cabin, crunching over shattered perspex, Otto pulled the pilot upright, his hands suddenly wet and sticky with the man's blood. The plane righted itself momentarily, for the Oberleutnant was still holding the controls.

'We're going to get you out!' he roared above the rush of the wind, holding himself to one side as perspex from the shattered window flew into his face like icy hailstones.

'No can do, old chap,' the pilot said in a tiny voice. 'Got to bite the bullet on this one . . . Had it . . . All . . . all buggered up.'

'Of course, you can!' Otto cried, angry with himself, the pilot, the whole damned war. 'Just let me get you out of this shitting harness . . .'

He stopped short. The pilot's head had fallen on one side, his mouth gaping open stupidly. By the green light that still came from the shattered instrument panel, Otto could now see the lazy curl of dark black blood which had begun to emerge from the man's slack lips. 'Herr Oberleutnant,' he cried desperately. 'Herr Oberleutnant, you can't go and die on us now!'

But even as he said the words he knew the pilot was dead. Next instant the Fieseler lurched yet again and Otto realized that there was nothing for it; the plane was lost; they were going to have to jump for it. He dropped his hold on the dead pilot's shoulder. There was no time for funeral orations now: for a drunk, he was a good man, but perhaps he ought to have stuck to removing silk knickers from obliging ladies of the night instead of flying. 'Count,' he cried, 'we've got to jump!'

'*How . . . jump?*'

Otto didn't wait for any further explanations. With all his strength, he ripped open the side panel of the cockpit, and a blast of icy air hit him with the force of a fist in the face. Down below he could see the pines racing by like a line of spike-helmeted soldiers on the march. Instinctively he knew they had only moments to save themselves; the ground was close enough as it was. In an instant the crippled plane would go into a nose dive and that would be that. Holding on as best he could with one hand, he reached out for the petrified Count.

'Come on – quick!'

'*Out?*'

'Yes, out!'

'*But . . . I've never done—*'

The Count's protests tailed off in a high-pitched scream as Otto pulled him to the open door and then, balancing like a professional acrobat, planted a massive kick in the other man's rear. In an instant the Count was out of the door and snatched up by the night. Otto flung a last glance at the pilot. There was no hope for him. He had to be left.

He stared down at the fleeting contours of forest, water, land. Suddenly horror overcame him. No sane man could do it. It wasn't possible. *He couldn't bring himself to jump!*

It was just then that the pilot's lifeless body slipped to the left, dragging the controls with him. The plane pitched alarmingly, and with a scream of absolute terror, Otto was flung out.

His head hit something. Red and white stars exploded in front of his eyes. For an instant he blacked out. When he came to, he found he was falling at a tremendous rate. With all his strength, fighting the pain in his head and the tremendous wind resistance, he grabbed the parachute-release handle on his chest. In a frenzy of fear, he pulled it.

Nothing happened!

Otto screamed. Then there was a crack. He felt a violent tug at his shoulders. Above him brilliant white silk erupted into the night sky, billowed out into a bubbling, confused flower and then – blessedly – formed itself miraculously into a perfect white canopy, halting his mad descent to destruction. Overcome by a feeling of absolute gratitude, he breathed out a tremendous sigh of relief. *He was saved . . . he was saved!*

But Otto's problems were far from over. The wind was blowing hard. He was being carried by it at high speed towards a wood on his right. He fumbled with the shroud-lines, but he had no idea how to use them to guide his descent. It was no use. He tensed his body, instinctively dragging up his legs to protect his abdomen, and held his breath, waiting for the moment of impact.

A group of spiked fir-tops came rushing up to meet him. He crashed into them the next moment. His nostrils were assailed by the almost overpowering odour of resin. Branches lashed his face cruelly. His chin smashed into something hard and rough. He blacked out.

How long he remained unconscious, Otto never knew.

When he came to, all was silence – a silence so profound and all-embracing that it seemed deafening.

He opened his eyes. Around him everything was white. Had it snowed while he had been unconscious? he asked himself in shocked surprise. Then he realized that he was swamped in his own silky-white parachute. Freeing himself from its folds, he looked up: above him now he could see the spiked outline of the fir-tops through which he had fallen. Somehow or other he must have navigated a path through them, for now he lay on the floor of the forest with pine-cones all about him.

Carefully, very carefully, fearing he might have broken a bone, he rose to his feet, the parachute falling about him like an abandoned skirt. His body felt as if it had been lashed by a whip and he could feel the soft trickle of blood on his face where the branches had torn at his skin. Thank God, no bones had been broken – once again luck had been on his side. But as soon as he freed himself from the parachute harness and took stock of his position he realized how absurd it was to talk of luck.

'*Luck!*' he cried out aloud in sudden despair. '*Luck, my arse!*' Suddenly he was overwhelmed by a sense of absolute, complete despair. He was alone in the middle of Russia. He didn't even know where he was. Like a pile of wet rags, shocked by that sudden revelation, he collapsed at the foot of a fir tree and lay there like a dead man, his eyes tightly closed . . .

FOUR

'I'm blind,' the strangely muffled voice said. 'Everything's gone black – black as a crow's back . . .'

Otto sat up startled, his every nerve-end tingling. There was someone out there, speaking German, however strange it sounded. Carefully, very carefully, he reached for his pistol. Hardly daring to breathe, he snapped off the safety-catch. The Popovs would never take him alive – he'd heard too many frightening stories about the feared NKVD Secret Police and their methods of interrogation.

Whoever it was out there in the dark forest blundered on, crashing through the trees like an ancient elephant, while Otto waited for the inevitable confrontation.

'I've always wondered what it would be like to be blind . . . Funnily enough, it doesn't seem very much different . . . There *must* be more to it than this, I expect . . . I suppose I *am* blind? I suppose I'll just have to get used to it . . .'

Otto's heart beat like a trip-hammer as the stranger drew closer, mumbling his absurd litany, and then the trees immediately to his front parted and a lone figure stood swaying there, his head monstrously distorted, hands groping blindly to his front as he sought to fight the importuning branches. Otto raised his pistol, his hand trembling like a leaf in spite of the fact that at that range he could hardly miss. Deliberately, forcing himself to be as calm as he could, he started to take aim.

The lone figure blundered a few metres closer, looming large and clear in Otto's sights. '*Now*,' he hissed to himself.

But just then his tension gave way to an almost hysterical outburst of laughter.

There was no mistaking the middle-aged figure standing there in the middle of the glade, his flying helmet pulled down over his eyes, muttering absurdly to himself. It was the Count!

'Herr Graf,' he called, barely able to restrain himself from screaming out loud with delight. 'It's Otto – Otto Stahl.'

The Count's hands groped blindly ahead of him. 'Otto, my dear boy, so you have survived too! How good it is to hear your voice again, although I am afraid to report that your old comrade is now gravely injured.' Like a blind man he fumbled Otto's sweat-lathered face with his hands. He lowered his voice, almost as if he were embarrassed by the confession. 'Don't be shocked, old friend, but . . . but—' there was a sob in his tone now, 'I am blind!'

Otto hastily stuck his pistol in his pocket and grabbed at the Count's helmet. 'Of course you're not blind, you silly shit!'

'But I *am*,' the Count persisted. 'When the plane hit the ground and exploded, there was a terrible flash right in front of me. The blast took my very breath away and that flash – it seemed to split my eyes open, right open—'

His monologue was cut short as Otto finally wrenched the thick, fur-lined helmet and cracked glasses from his face, leaving him blinking uneasily in the darkness, with the cold night breeze whisking away the sweat from his forehead and nose. 'I say, you're right, Otto,' he stuttered, 'I'm not blind at all.' He rubbed his eyes, as if unable to believe this sudden miracle. 'How – how did you do it, Otto?'

'Oh, knock it off,' Otto said. Although his tone was disgruntled, secretly his heart was jumping with joy at the knowledge that he was no longer alone in this vast alien place. 'So the plane bought it, did it?'

'Yes,' the Count said, sitting down on the turf with a sigh

of relief. 'I suppose I could have coped with being blind. People are very sympath—'

'So,' Otto cut him short, 'if the Popovs find the plane or what's left of it, they'll probably think it was some lone German plane which had strayed over their frontier by mistake?'

'Yes, you could be right there, Otto. I don't think they have any reason to suspect that we were running a mission into Mother Russia. On the other hand they are a very suspicious people.'

For a moment or two the two of them sat in silence in the lonely glade, considering their position, the only sound the hiss of the wind in the swaying tree-tops and the cry of the lonely night-birds.

It was Otto who finally broke the heavy stillness. 'You realize, Count, don't you, that we have gone and landed ourselves with our hooters right down in the crap once more. It seems to be – what did that poor old fly-boy call it? – standard operating procedure for the two of us.'

'Yes,' the Count replied, eminently calm once more. 'We are rather in the ordure, or so it would seem. But *nil desperandum* – all is not lost, I can assure you. I well recall as a boy, for example, how we once had a vet on my father's estate in East Prussia who tended our animals when they were ailing. A strange man – he had rather obscure theories about the treatment of the herd, I seem to recall. One day we had an old Holstein cow with some sort of internal trouble – the kind of thing he always interpreted as gas. In order to investigate, he stuck one of his rubber tubes up the animal's – er – anus, if you'll forgive the term, and as it was rather dark in the barn, he struck a match to see exactly what he was doing. The animal broke wind. The gas ignited, and a two-metre flame shot from its anus. The flame set light to some hay nearby. The barn caught on fire and my father had to suffer damages estimated, in the end, at five hundred gold marks. The Holstein, let me say, escaped with a shock, though my father never employed the vet again.'

Otto looked at his companion incredulously. 'Have you got all your cups in yer cupboard?' he breathed in awe. 'Have you got air in your tooth? Have you got a little bird in yer head that goes peep-peep? In short, Count, *are you cracked?* In three devils' name what *are* you trying to tell me with that crazy story?'

The Count was unmoved by Otto's angry outburst. 'This, my dear boy. We must expect the unexpected. We approach a thing one way and it ends in a completely different manner than anticipated. Casualties do occur – my father's barn and our unfortunate pilot, for example – but the chief protagonists escape to fight another day.'

'You mean the vet and the Holstein?'

'Exactly.'

'You make a fine comparison – a shitting cow and a dummy who spends his time poking tubes up animals' arses! But go on, get on with it.'

The Count beamed at him. 'So, we have experienced an unpleasant surprise. The mission has not turned out as anticipated – they never do really, do they? So we must try another approach.'

Now Otto's face lit up too. 'You mean, Count,' he asked eagerly, 'that we're to hoof it back to the frontier? Get out of this mess while we've still got a chance?'

'Not exactly, my boy.'

Otto's happy look vanished as quickly as it had come.

'*Back* we are going to go, Otto, naturally. But first we must execute the task that General Dietrich has entrusted to us. We are in rather the same position as Robinson Crusoe, when he first realized that he was alone on his island and that somehow or other he would have to survive. He counted his resources – his powder, his musket, his tins of biscuit, and so on. We must do the same and consider how best to exploit them.'

'What resources?' Otto asked, in a voice heavy with despair.

'We have our pistols.'

Otto nodded.

'We have five hundred rubles apiece; that is, one thousand between the two of us. Please remember, your average collective-farm peasant earns at the most five rubles a day. We are in possession of a minor fortune, in other words.'

Again Otto said nothing.

'And most importantly of all, we have our intelligence,' the Count concluded.

'And what can we do with that intelligence?'

'We can work out how we can still carry out the mission that General Dietrich gave us. The offensive, as you know, starts on June 22nd. Today is June 18th. So we have four days in which to find out what he wants to know and get back to our own lines – a matter of,' the Count shrugged eloquently, 'a mere fifty kilometres or so.'

'*A mere fifty kilometres or so*,' Otto mimicked his tone bitterly. 'On Shanks' pony, with no Popov pass? You do recall, don't you, that in the workers' and peasants' paradise one needs such a thing to move from village to village? And there's a well-defended frontier to cross!'

'Difficulties are there to be overcome, my young friend,' replied the Count. And with that he fell silent.

Otto knew that his old running-mate had made up his mind. He would never turn back from his self-imposed task now; indeed, he would probably go it alone, if necessary. It would be no use trying to humour him. The best he could do was to save the old fool from himself.

'All right,' he said finally, 'all right. Let's cut the time down from four to three days – to exactly seventy-two hours. No matter how thick they are, sooner or later the Popovs will tumble to the fact that our troops massing back there on the frontier haven't come to play *skat* with their dear Russian comrades. They'll seal the border up as tight

as a nun's knees. Seventy-two hours – *einverstanden?*' He
looked hard at the Count in the darkness, but could make
out no change in his expression.

'Agreed!'

'Good. We'll have to travel cross-country under difficult
conditions at night – and with your paunch, Count, I
reckon the most we can cover is twenty-five klicks a day.
So we've got exactly two days to cover the way back to the
frontier. *Einverstanden?*'

'Agreed!'

'Which means we've got twenty-four hours to find out
what that Bavarian barn-shitter Dietrich wants to know
about the Miropol Position. *Twenty-four hours*, no more, no
less. *Einverstanden?*'

'Agreed!'

'So, my dear Count, I don't want you to go ape-shit in
any way. If we don't achieve our objective within twenty-
four hours, we turn back just like that,' he snapped his
thumb and forefinger, 'and no messing.' He flashed a
glance at the green-glowing dial of his wrist-watch.
'All right, circumsize yer time-piece! It is now precisely two
o'clock on the morning of June 19th, 1941. If we're not on
target by two o'clock on the 20th, we make dust back to the
frontier as quick as we can go.'

'Agreed!' The Count reached over and shook his companion's hand warmly. 'Otto,' he said enthusiastically,
'you have made the right decision. There will be fame and
honour for us at last.'

Wearily, Otto rose to his feet. 'I shit on fame and
honour, Count,' he said grumpily as his friend followed
suit. 'All Mrs Stahl's handsome son wants to do is to live
to see June 22nd, 1942.'

'A not unreasonable aim,' the Count answered. Then
the two of them set off. Moments later the silver gloom
had swallowed them up as if they had never existed.

FIVE

The loathsome thing lay hunched behind the shattered controls of the burned-out plane like a wrinkled pygmy, its teeth gleaming a bright obscene-white in wizened, skull-like features.

The peasants and the soldiers who herded them back from the site of the crash, stared at it with fascinated revulsion. Occasionally, the older ones among them would surreptitiously cross themselves and whisper prayers to the Black Virgin of Kazan, even though such things were a punishable offence.

Todleben stood beside his staff car and stared at the scene, too: the charred grass, the wrecked trees, ripped apart by the plane in its last dive, their branches lying on the freshly churned-up earth like severed limbs; the absurd *Kolhoz* peasants in their ragged clothes, and the babbling, ignorant militia. He saw them and yet he did not. His mind's eye was on a single image: that of the crooked cross on the wrecked plane's tail.

The swastika. The sign of the fascist beast. What was a Fritz plane doing here so far behind Russian lines?

Around him staff, all of them armed with tommy-guns and wearing the dreaded green cross emblem of the NKVD in their caps, waited too. But their eyes were not on the plane, the crowd, the scene of the wreck; their eyes were fixed on their chief, Colonel Todleben, ready to spring into action immediately he gave an order. For it did not pay to be laggard where Todleben was concerned. More than one NKVD officer serving under him had vanished into the camps of the Gulag Archipelago.

He was a tall man, rather like his famous ancestor, the Baltic–German in the Imperial Service who had played such an important role in the defence of Sevastopol against those cur-dogs, the English, when they had invaded Mother Russia nearly a century before. But there the resemblance ended. His descendant's face was strikingly handsome in a rather pretty Georgian manner – straight nose, very full, dark-red lips, and a woman's cheeks. There were rumours of handsome boys who visited him in his rooms and were never seen or heard of again. But those were matters that his staff hardly dared so much as think about, for Colonel Todleben, Head of the NKVD in Southern Russia, had two of the coldest and cruellest eyes ever seen – even among the professional sadists of the feared Secret Police. Todleben was an icy-hearted killer to whom human life meant nothing and the cause of Soviet Russia everything.

For the first time since they had reached the site of the mysterious crash, Todleben moved. He shrugged his shoulders. Immediately, two members of his staff rushed forward and removed his ankle-length coat, for now the sun was beginning to flush the sky a blood-red hue in the east – a sure sign of another very hot day. Todleben tossed aside the long *papyrokki* he had been smoking and gestured to left and right with his elegantly manicured hand.

The staff jumped into action at once. '*Davoi* . . . *davoi* . . .' they cried, pushing into the crowd of gawping peasants and awed barefoot militia. 'Clear the way for Comrade Colonel Todleben . . . *Davoi*, you lice-ridden peasant scum . . .'

Hastily the crowd fell back, all eyes fixed now on the tall, elegant figure standing on the rise next to the big black limousine, his gaze fixed on some distant object visible only to him.

'Comrade Colonel, the way is clear!' Petrov, the next senior officer reported, standing rigidly to attention, hand touching his cap in salute. Imperiously, Todleben strode forward, the dust swirling up around his gleaming top-boots, his hawk-like nose wrinkled a little at the strong smell of unwashed bodies emanating from the awed crowd of peasants and militia. He peered closely at the hideous figure of the pilot, staring at the repulsive thing without the least sign of horror, then clicked his fingers.

Petrov knew immediately what Todleben wanted. He sprang forward, trying not to look at the charred Fritz, and tendered the freshly laundered handkerchief which he always kept ready for his chief. Todleben accepted it without a word and held it in his palm expectantly. Petrov gulped, a little overcome by the stench of the corpse, and hastily unscrewing the flask of eau-de-cologne, poured some on the square of cloth.

Delicately, Todleben patted the scented cloth to his nostrils, while everyone waited in awe for his pronouncement. Finally it came. 'Secure the area – I want the others!' he ordered in a thin, almost feminine voice.

'The others?' Petrov gasped. Although he had long thought he had become accustomed to the moods, whims, and flashes of intuition which had made Todleben the most successful NKVD officer outside of Moscow and a favourite of that other monster, Beria,[1] this Petrov was quite unable to follow his chief's line of thought.

'Yes,' Todleben said slowly, as if he were formulating not only his words but also his thoughts as he spoke. 'The pilot wasn't alone. Look at the door.' He indicated the frame-and-wood door which hung crazily from one hinge. 'It has been forced from the inside. You may be quite sure, my dear Petrov, that the pilot had nothing to do with the forcing of it, eh?'

'Naturally, Comrade Colonel.'

'Look there, too.' Todleben indicated the sandy earth of the Rumanian landing-strip, which unwittingly Otto and the Count had brought into the plane with them as they crossed the ground soaked by the bottles the drunken

[2] Head of the NKVD.

Luftwaffe mechanics had upset in the darkness. 'There were others with him – perhaps two of them, to judge by the space available in this kind of plane.'

Suddenly Todleben reached and grabbed the charred horror by the hair, which lay on the dead man's skull like fused, blackened wire. The crowd gave an audible gasp. Next to Todleben, Petrov felt the hot green bile well up into his throat and threaten to choke him. He swallowed hastily, his face suddenly ochre-coloured.

Todleben's handsome features revealed no emotion other than burning curiosity. 'You see that, Petrov?' he said, pointing to the little cross which had been welded into the dead pilot's throat like a jewel worn by some Hindu *hoori* in her navel.

Petrov nodded, unable to speak.

'Do you know what it is?'

'No, Comrade,' he answered thickly.

'Then I shall tell you,' Todleben said, still holding the ghastly head in his elegant hand, like a professor of anatomy lecturing a class of hard-boiled medical students. 'It is what the Fritzes call the Knight's Cross of the Iron Cross. For the fascists it is a very high decoration, awarded only to the most experienced and the bravest of their soldiers. Now, Comrade Petrov, is it likely that such an experienced pilot would fly so far off course as to cross into Soviet territory? On a perfect night like last night?'

'Not really, Comrade Colonel.'

'Further,' Todleben continued, 'what was an aviator of that calibre doing piloting this collection of plywood, canvas and catgut, eh?' He fixed Petrov with those cold green eyes of his. 'Pray tell me that, Petrov.' He let the head fall. It hit the shattered controls and split down the centre of the skull like an over-ripe coconut. Something white and obscenely pink began to seep from the back of the dead German's skull.

Petrov swallowed desperately, but Todleben's face remained perfectly calm. In the crowd the peasants were crossing themselves furiously, as if their lives depended upon it, and the more impressionable of the younger women were burying their humble peasant faces in their aprons in the old Russian manner.

'Well, Petrov?' Todleben demanded.

'Some sort of mission . . .' Petrov heard himself stutter, as if he were listening to another man's voice entirely.

'*Some sort of mission,*' Todleben sneered and held out his hands. Hastily Petrov poured eau-de-cologne over them, trying to keep his gaze off that oozing skull, his hands trembling violently as he did so. 'I shall tell you what that mission is. It is the same as all the missions that the foreigners have run into our country ever since 1917. Whatever their guise, the objective is always the same – *espionage and sabotage aimed at undermining the security of our country!*'

Petrov looked at his superior and for the very first time saw real emotion on his cruelly handsome face. Todleben, who in Petrov's eyes at least, was a foreigner himself, really believed in what he said: that Russia's ruination was caused by foreign machinations. Petrov, however, was careful not to let his master know his own true feelings, which were that Soviet Russia had been ruined not by outsiders, but by the bunglings of her own masters. Instead he said, 'And where will this espionage and sabotage be carried out, Comrade Colonel?'

'I do not know exactly, Petrov, but this much is clear – there are two mouthless ones—' he used the old Russian word for Germans '—who perhaps do not speak our language and who undoubtedly will not have the necessary *papruski*[3] for travelling between one place and another and who will be moving on foot somewhere within a radius of . . .' he made a quick calculation '. . . fifteen kilometres of here, southwards perhaps, but more likely heading towards the east in order to execute their criminal mission.'

---

[4] Papers.

He paused and glared at the smaller man. 'I don't doubt that you will find them, Petrov. Or . . .'

Petrov snapped to attention, fear tracing an icy finger down his spine at the unspoken threat. 'Naturally, Comrade Colonel! Of course, Comrade Colonel! With luck I shall have apprehended them by nightfall. There is nothing to fear. I shall ensure that everything that you wish will be done.'

Todleben smiled at him. 'It always is, Petrov.' With that he strode back to his car. But before he got in, he paused to beckon to a barefoot youth with wide innocent blue eyes beneath a thatch of flaxen hair. 'Would you like a caramel, boy?' he said, his voice suddenly very husky, eyes greedy.

The boy nodded, moving awkwardly from one bare foot to the other in the white dust.

Carefully, Colonel Todleben took out from his pocket one of the caramels which he always carried with him and unwrapped it for the waiting child, while the group of peasants looked on in awe. He held it high, as one might do a titbit for a favourite dog. 'Hold up your head, pretty boy,' he breathed.

The boy stretched back his head, his mouth wide open to reveal brilliant white teeth, his little pink tongue hanging out. Delicately, very delicately, Todleben placed the caramel on the tip of the boy's tongue, commanding, 'Suck it slowly, very slowly indeed, with the utmost of pleasure . . .'

Seconds later he was back in his limousine and away in a cloud of white dust, leaving Petrov staring after him, hands bunched to fists at his sides, his face flushed with a sudden burning rage. One day, thought Petrov, when the revolution finally came, that pervert Todleben would be the first to feel the cold muzzle of his pistol at the base of his skull. It would be a pleasure to blast him to hell, his final destination.

SIX

All through that first night Otto and the Count had marched, heading eastwards as best they could, but guided more by intuition than knowledge. Towards dawn, when they saw the first villages appear in the steppe before them, heralded by lazy blue smoke curling into the still morning air and the barking of the mangy village dogs, they had gone to ground, dozing uneasily in the hot sun and waking up that same evening with burning headaches and tongues like old leather.

As soon as the last red rays of the setting sun had disappeared below the horizon, they were on their way again. A river had barred their progress and they had plunged into it greedily, drinking and swimming at the same time, grateful for the new strength it had given their parched, dehydrated bodies. An hour later they had stumbled upon a field of water melons some half a kilometre outside a small collective farm, and had gorged themselves on the ripe, cool fruit – though not without effect. As Otto had commented after their fourth sudden halt: 'I expected to fight across Russia, but I didn't expect to crap myself across it!'

'Perhaps that is what the Englishmen mean by keeping a stiff upper lip, eh!' the Count had replied with a laugh. Otto had not even bothered to comment.

By dawn the following morning they had reached greener, softer countryside, broken here and there by vineyards surrounded by low, dry stone walls; occasionally they also came across wells which poured water into stone channels as a means of irrigation, and which, as the Count commented, would make an ideal defensive position 'for a handful of determined infantrymen'.

As Otto absorbed the information, his eyes were already fixed on the high plateau to their front, which was shimmering in little blue ripples as the first heat haze of that burningly hot day descended upon the plain. Here the steep ridged slopes were barren and stony, devoid of vines.

Although he was no soldier, Otto instinctively knew that ahead of them lay the Miropol Position. If the Popovs were going to defend the limitless steppe which stretched right up to the Rumanian frontier some fifty kilometres behind them, it would be here.

'Count,' he announced, as the sun finally thrust itself over the height in its full brazen glory, 'I think we're there. We'd better go to ground.'

The Count had slumped wearily into the cover of the vines, whose branches formed into rough figures of eight so that the grapes would capture the maximum amount of sun. 'Otto, I think you're right. If any place is going to be Miropol, it's up there.'

Otto nodded. Within five minutes he was fast asleep.

When they awoke it was blessedly cool again and although the still unripe grapes were sour, they stilled the two men's thirst. Now they were ready to complete the final stage of their mission.

In silence they plodded ever closer to the forbidding height of the plateau, now outlined a stark black against the warm velvet of the night sky. The going was tough, and Otto could hear the older man panting hard, but neither he nor the Count thought of taking a break. Both knew instinctively that if this was the Miropol Position they were in danger every minute they lingered; the first priority was to get in, find out what they wanted to know and then be gone as quickly as possible.

Now they encountered a series of low stone walls, but even in the darkness Otto could see they were not the rough-stone ones built by the peasants; these were made of concrete. 'Outer defensive position, Count?' he queried in a whisper.

'Think so, my boy. And look there – concertina wire. I think we've found it!'

They pushed on, skirting three-metre-high rolls of barbed wire and slipping off to the left into a kind of small wood of coarse prickly gorse that ripped at their hands as they parted it. For the time being they didn't mind the pain – at least the gorse wasn't as bad as the wire, which they would have found impossible to get through without special tools.

Five minutes passed, and they plodded on. Another five. Now a soft yellow sickle moon had appeared in the sky and was bathing the stark terrain below in its gentle light. They pushed on more rapidly, able to see where they were going now. The gorse bushes began to peter out. Otto wiped the sweat off his forehead with a scratched and bloody hand. 'Over there, Count – it looks like some sort of a path out of these shitty things,' he whispered.

The Count nodded his agreement. 'But be careful. Paths might be covered – and watch out for trip-wires.'

In single file, bodies crouched low and tense, their nerve-ends jangling, both of them half-expecting the harsh challenge which would spell disaster, they crept cautiously along the stony path. Then suddenly the Count stopped. Otto just avoided stumbling into him at the very last moment. 'What the hell—'

His angry words died on his lips as he, too, saw what had startled the Count. 'Oh, my aching arse!' he breathed in open-mouthed wonder. 'What in three devils' name is that?'

The Count swallowed hard and stared up at the monstrous gun barrel that towered up in front of them, its breech disappearing into a low concrete bunker, its roof camouflaged with soil and covered with gorse bushes identical to the ones they had just fought their way through. 'It's a long time since I saw anything like *that*, Otto – to be exact, in front of Verdun in '16 in the last war when the Bavarians brought up the biggest Krupp cannon they could muster to pound Fort Vaux. My guess is that that one's an ex-battleship gun, perhaps with a calibre of – say – twelve point five centimetres.'

'It's en . . .normous!' Otto stuttered. 'And look, Count, over there, there's another of them . . . and another . . .'

They spent the next five minutes crawling along the height, which seemed strangely deserted though the air was heavy with the characteristic smell of Russian humanity – unwashed bodies, garlic and black *marhorka* tobacco. Obviously there were Russian soldiers about somewhere. Finally they slipped beneath the cover of a gorse bush, satisfied that they had found out all they could in the darkness.

'Five of them altogether,' the Count whispered, and wiped the sweat off his high forehead, 'all with a range of twenty to twenty-five kilometres, I'd say.'

'As much as that?'

'Yes, as much as that,' the Count said firmly.

'Heaven, arse and cloudburst, they'll make mincemeat of old Dietrich's flat-foot guards! They won't know what's hit them! And besides, they're far too well camouflaged for the fly-boys to take out.'

'Stukas?' the Count said hopefully.

'Those warm brothers! They're all right for frightening a lot of old grannies and kids, but for real they couldn't piss in a pot accurately!'

'It'll be the end of the Bodyguard,' the Count said solemnly. 'It'll be a massacre. They'll never be able to get within killing distance—' Suddenly he stopped short and gripped Otto's arm, hard. Instinctively Otto turned his gaze in the direction indicated by his companion.

A dark silhouette had detached itself from the gloomy shadow cast by the nearest gun turret. Otto could just make out the silver glint of his long bayonet.

'Sentry?' he hissed.

The Count nodded his head, not taking his eyes off the figure as the man advanced slowly in their direction. They froze, hardly daring to breathe. Would he never stop? If he continued on his present path, he would blunder right into them. Their only cover was the shadow cast by the bush under which they were crouching. Otto felt his throat constrict. In a minute they would be discovered, and it wouldn't take the Popovs long to discover what they were doing there. By dawn they'd be lining them up against the wall of some stinking backyard in front of a firing squad.

Suddenly the man stopped, a mere five metres away from them. *Had he spotted them?* Otto waited for the inevitable. Nothing happened. Instead the sentry ripped open his breeches and gave a sigh of relief as he released a hot stream of urine onto the baked, stony earth. At that moment Otto felt very much like doing the same.

Lazily, like sentries all over the world with nothing much to do and a long spell of boring guard duty in front of them, the Russian soldier did up his breeches, while the two men hidden only metres away in the shadows waited with frantic impatience. Finally he was finished with the operation. But still he didn't go back to the spot from whence he had come. Instead, Otto and the Count heard the rasp of a match on a hard surface and in the sudden spurt of blue flame, caught a quick glimpse of a yellow, slant-eyed, youthful face; then the flame went out and they could hear the gasp of pleasure as the sentry breathed out a stream of blue smoke. Still he didn't move!

The Count pressed his mouth close to Otto's mouth. 'What now?'

For a moment, Otto, the quick-witted product of the Berlin slums, was stumped. As long as the sentry remained where he was, they couldn't move back through the gorse without attracting his attention. Yet they couldn't stop here much longer. Sooner or later they would be discovered. Time was running out.

Otto pressed his mouth close to the other man's ear. 'We've got to nobble him,' he said – but with a sense of inner bitterness and failure, for he had sworn in 1939 never to hurt a fellow human being if he could help it; yet, as always, he was in another situation where he had to hurt in order to save his own skin. 'There's no other way. Count, can you attract his attention, and I'll—' Otto bit his lip '—deal with him.'

The Count nodded.

'Give me exactly sixty seconds. *Klar?*'

Gingerly, very gingerly, covering the stony earth millimetre by millimetre, Otto felt his way up the path, groping for any loose stone that might betray his presence and counting off the sixty seconds as he went. By the time the minute was up, he was lying stretched across the path on his back, the tell-tale white blur of his face hidden, or so he hoped, by the shadow cast by a gorse bush. With a bit of luck the sentry might take him for a fallen log. '*Sixty,*' he breathed urgently to himself, and tensed.

'I say, my man, excuse me, please!' The Count's voice broke the tense silence.

Otto almost groaned out loud. The silly old fool sounded like some upper-class chinless wonder trying to attract the attention of a policeman in Berlin's *Unter den Linden*. But the call seemed to do the trick. The sentry straightened up, startled, and the glowing butt of his cigarette dropped from his fingers. '*Stoi?*' he challenged, fumbling urgently for his rifle. '*Stoi?*'

'Have you got a moment?' the Count continued.

Otto tensed. He could hear the click as the Russian nervously removed his safety-catch. If he fired there and then, that would be it. They'd be lost. But apparently the sentry wasn't the firing kind. Instead, he repeated his challenge and stepped forward. Otto held his free hand ready. With the other he clutched his clubbed pistol, its muzzle already wet with his own sweat.

'*Stoi?*' the Russian repeated nervously, halting a metre away.

Inwardly Otto groaned. The Popov prick was just out of reach. '*Move*,' he muttered under his breath, willing the suspicious young soldier to cover that last metre.

Suddenly the Count gave a dramatic groan, as if about to faint, and Otto heard him crashing to the ground, tearing aside the bushes.

The Count's ploy succeeded. The Russian darted forward. Otto grabbed for his foot and twisted hard. The Russian yelped with pain and came tumbling down, bayonet flying from his hands, body falling on Otto.

Desperately the German squirmed to free himself. With all his strength he lashed out with the clubbed pistol – but missed. Realizing the danger he was in, the Russian tried to scramble up. Otto jammed his elbow into the man's stomach. The Russian gasped with pain and surprise, and fell again. Immediately Otto was on top of him, his hands grabbing frantically for the terrified soldier's throat to prevent him from calling out. They connected. The Russian's body arched wildly. It took all Otto's strength to keep his sweat-lathered hands around the Russian's neck as he thrashed and whipped from side to side to break the killing hold.

'For Christ's sake, be quiet!' Otto called through gritted teeth. 'I won't hurt you, if you just don't shout out!'

But the Russian, even if he had understood German, was too carried away by fear to obey and continued to writhe furiously, strange, meaningless sounds coming from his gaping mouth. Frantic with fear and rage, Otto increased his pressure on the Russian's throat and leaned back to obtain more strength, employing all his back muscles, his legs pinning the Russian to the ground. Remorselessly his fingers dug deeper and deeper into the soft flesh of his neck. Carried away by a mindless, atavistic blood-rage, everything in front of his bulging eyes a roaring red, he pressed and pressed and pressed, ignoring the last frenzied arching of the spine, the strange bubbling, plopping noises that came from the other man's mouth and the sudden, strange limpness of his body – all that counted was to *press . . . press . . . press . . . forever . . . press . . .*

'*Otto!*' An urgent voice seemed to come from far, far away. 'Otto, stop! He's dead . . . *dead*, I tell you.'

A hand grasped his shoulder roughly and he felt himself being shaken as a mother might shake a very naughty child. He shook his head, as if he were waking up out of a deep and horrible nightmare. A yellow face, now flushed with blood, stared up at him. He recoiled with horror. Frantically he pulled his hands away, and they made a dreadful sucking noise as they parted from the wet flesh of the dead man. 'What did you say?' he croaked.

Roughly the Count hauled him to his feet. 'He's dead, Otto – can't you see?'

'My God, no,' Otto said, his voice full of pleading. 'Don't say that! I only wanted to quieten him . . . Not kill . . .'

Gently now, the Count took the trembling young man by the hand. 'Come on, Otto. There's nothing more you can do about it . . . Come, come with me.'

Numbly, Otto let himself be led away, the tears streaming down his sweat-lathered face. Behind him the man he had killed started to stiffen rapidly in the cool night air.

SEVEN

'Beretta pistol, you say, Petrov?' Todleben's voice was metallic and strangely distorted over the artillerymen's field telephone.

'Yes, Comrade Colonel,' Petrov answered dutifully. In the background the gunners manning the bunkers started to carry away the dead man to be buried at the back of the Miropol Position. 'Whoever killed the sentry must have lost it in the confusion of the fight.'

'The Macaronis are the fascist Germans' allies. It could well be that one of their agents would use an Italian weapon.'

'Very likely, Comrade Colonel,' Petrov agreed hastily. As always with the tyrant Todleben, he told him what he wanted to hear.

'Anything else?'

'Two lots of footprints, Comrade, heading away down the hillside from the scene of the crime. Judging by the way the earth was disturbed it also seems that they had been scouting the whole Miropol Position.'

'Of course, of course. Surely even a person of your limited intelligence, Petrov, must realize what their mission was – to spy out our guns. That's why they were there.'

'Yes, Comrade Colonel,' Petrov answered, his face burning a deep crimson. To make matters worse, he was sure that the tall, intellectual-looking artillery colonel standing next to him in the office had heard Todleben's comment.

'*Yes, Comrade Colonel!*' Todleben mimicked cruelly. 'Is that all you can ever say, Petrov? Are you just a yes-man?

56

I hope not, because there are plenty of other able young officers eager for the position you hold, you know. No one is indispensable.'

Next to him the tall artilleryman with the gold-rimmed pince-nez and the emaciated face winked slowly. But Petrov was relieved to see there was no malice in the wink; it was meant benevolently. The man obviously knew what overbearing, sadistic monsters their leaders were.

Petrov flashed him a thin smile, although as an NKVD officer he knew he should have frowned on such attempts at 'fraternization', as it was officially classed in the NKVD's *'Rules of Conduct'*.

'No, Comrade Colonel,' Petrov replied in answer to his master's question, 'that is *not* all I have done. I have alerted the whole of the Southern Region to be on the lookout for two Germans, one of them armed, both presumably young, and wearing dirty, tattered clothes – the result of crawling around here among the gorse-bushes. I have also recruited the assistance of the Red Army, and the Fifth Red Cossack Cavalry Division has placed its riders at my disposal. They are already out scouring the area in search of the two murderers. Further, I have contacted our office at Brest-Litovsk and requested that the whole border from Poland down to Rumania should be sealed off. I do not know as yet whether a decision has been made on that matter, Comrade.'

Todleben was impressed. 'You have done well, Comrade Major,' he said grudgingly; being Todleben, however, he hated ending on a positive note. 'But you must ensure that there is no loophole through which these criminals can escape. We must assume that they are highly trained professionals, resourceful, hard men who know what they are about. Watch for the loophole, Comrade Petrov! *Dosvedanya.*' And with that he hung up, leaving Petrov glaring at the clumsy, old-fashioned field telephone.

Opposite him, the Artillery Colonel winked again. 'Come

the day of the revolution, blood will flow and heads roll, eh, comrade?'

Grimly Petrov nodded, knowing again that he was encouraging 'fraternization', and said, 'Of that you can be sure, comrade. The heads will certainly roll . . . or, at least, *one* in particular . . .' Then he forgot Todleben and started concentrating on that loophole. What and where could it be? Through what possible loophole could a fugitive escape in the gigantic Gulag that was Soviet Russia?

'A noble beast, the horse,' the Count said, patting the matted mane of his flea-bitten old nag, which was sagging at the belly under his weight. 'I had really quite forgotten the pleasure a good horse can give to a man.'

'Pleasure!' Otto groaned, shifting his weight yet again and feeling the fiery soreness between his legs. 'But still, it's better than walking, I suppose.' Beneath him, his own horse gave a weary sigh, as if it couldn't wait for the end of this interminable ride.

The purchase of the horses had been surprisingly easy. At first, Otto had been against the plan, but after walking most of the morning, he had finally been persuaded when they met a barefoot peasant-boy leading two old nags out into the fields. With many gestures and the Count's few words of Russian, they had made it clear to the youth that they wished to buy the horses from him. Of course, they didn't know it, but the horses didn't belong to him at all – they belonged to the collective farm on which his parents worked. The sight of the two twenty-rouble pieces had soon convinced the boy that the Five Year Plan would still be able to function without these particular two horses, and he had grabbed the money and run off gleefully to inform his parents that two strange men had offered him a small fortune for something that hadn't belonged to him in the first place. Of course, when the headman questioned them about the horses' disappearance, they would have to make up some tale or other about how they had been stolen.

Within the hour the two precious gold pieces had been buried deep beneath the floor of their little wooden cottage and mother, father and son were alarming the entire surrounding countryside with their wailing cries that a great theft had taken place.

But all this was, of course, unknown to Otto and the Count as they plodded steadily westwards on their mounts, heading for the far blue blur which was the mountain range that lay in Rumania. The plan was simple. They would ride the horses until they reached the frontier zone. Then they would abandon them and approach as close as they dared on foot, in order to ascertain the depth of the Russian positions and the best means of slipping through them. With luck they would be able to get through that same night.

As always, the Count had made it all seem very easy – he was a man who was constitutionally incapable of seeing problems and difficulties; but all the same, Otto knew it was as good a plan as any. Besides, the Russian countryside was strangely deserted: all this long afternoon they had seen only two small hamlets in the distance in spite of the obvious fertility of the earth; it could well be that the frontier would be equally sparsely defended.

About three o'clock that long, hot afternoon, just as they had begun to walk the tired nags up a long incline to give them a breather, they had their first sign of trouble, in the form of an ancient Rata biplane. Out of nowhere, it came winging its way low across the burning steppe with the sun behind it, so that for a moment or two all they could do was shield their eyes from the glare. And then it was flashing overhead, blocking out the sun momentarily so that they could see the bright red stars underneath its wings, and dragging its shadow behind it like some giant evil raven. Moments later it was climbing steeply into the burning blue sky, heading westwards.

Otto stopped and looked at the Count. 'Are you thinking what I am, Count?'

Grimly, without his usual jaunty smile, the Count nodded. 'Yes, definitely a military plane.'

'And definitely looking for us?'

Again the Count nodded.

'What now?'

'I think, Otto, my dear boy, we ought to mount up, ride our horses into the ground and then, when they can't go any further, continue on foot. Speed is essential.'

'Agreed,' Otto said, fumbling for his stirrup. 'But I tell you, my arse has never burnt like this since the day old Herold, my teacher, walloped it for looking up the skirt of the new domestic science teacher.' With a groan he lowered himself into the saddle and his mount sagged, as if about to sink to the ground. Otto slapped its moth-eaten, skinny rump, 'Come on, or I'll send you to the glue factory, toot-sweet!' The threat seemed to work. The old nag started to move forward once again.

One hour later, the Count looked back. As he spoke, the alarm in his voice was unmistakable. 'Otto, they're there!'

Otto swung around. A line of small, dark shapes seemed to have appeared on the ridge to their rear. By squinting against the glare he could just make out tiny flashes of sparkling silver. They could only come from polished equipment. 'Soviet cavalry?' he queried, knowing the answer even before the Count gave it.

'Yes, I'm afraid so, Otto.' The Count flashed a glance at the sun, which now hung like a blood orange on the burning horizon, as if it were hesitating before allowing night to fall. 'But in another hour it'll be dark. If we can keep ahead of them till then, I reckon we stand a chance.'

'Come on, then – what are we waiting for!' Otto cried, and dug his heels into his mount. 'I'm not letting some hairy-arsed Cossack stick his spear into me!'

Now they started to whip the last reserves of strength out of their tired nags, spurred to cruelty by the knowledge that this might be their last chance of escaping the enemy cavalry. But as the June sun slipped ever further behind the horizon – with maddening slowness, or so it seemed to them – the Soviet cavalry came closer and closer. At first the distance between the two groups of riders was three or four kilometres; then it narrowed down to a kilometre-and-a-half; and by the time the first dark shadows of the night came sliding across the steppe, clothing it in blessed purple darkness at last, the two fugitives could hear the clatter of hooves behind them quite clearly.

Now both they and their mounts were lathered in sweat, the horses breathing harshly as if in the throes of some fatal asthmatic attack. Still the two fugitives urged them on, digging their knees and heels savagely into their heaving, gleaming flanks, cursing the unfortunate animals bitterly, carried away by their unreasoning fear.

Crack! A slug howled through the air and a spurt of sandy soil erupted just to the front of the Count's horse. It shied, but the Count yanked the bit cruelly into its mouth. The horse whinnied piteously, but raced on.

Otto flung a glance behind him. Fear overcame him. They were Cossacks all right. He could even see the black uniforms and the fur hats set at jaunty angles on the riders' heads as they stretched the lengths of their mounts' flying manes, firing as they rode. Wild, cruel faces stared greedily at him. God knows what would happen to them if they fell into the hands of those fierce, half-wild cavalrymen. 'The pistol!' he screamed above the clatter of their horses' hooves.

'What?'

'*The shitting pistol . . . quick!*'

The Count understood. Whipping out their sole remaining weapon, he tossed it butt forward to the younger man. By some miracle, Otto caught it. He didn't hesitate. Swinging round in the saddle, he fired wildly. He was lucky. His first slug hit the leading rider. Otto saw him throw up his arms and drop his reins. For what seemed an age he seemed suspended thus, a thin, never-ending wail coming from his bearded lips. Then he disappeared from sight, his horse racing on, caught up by the excitement of the chase, riderless now.

There were angry shouts from behind them and another slug howled through the darkening air to whine off a rock to their right. They galloped on.

Now a downhill slope stretched ahead of the two fugitives. Frantically they urged their mounts down it. To their right, some five hundred metres away, there was some kind of wood. Once there, Otto reasoned, they stood a chance of giving their pursuers the slip. It was getting darker by the moment now. But first they had to reach it.

'The wood, Count,' he gasped, crouching low over the gleaming neck of his horse, 'try to get to it! Jump the nag and make a run for it! Understood?'

'Understood, Otto!'

Otto turned once more. The Cossacks were beginning to catch up again. Somehow or other he had the fleeting impression that there were fewer of them now, but the fact barely registered. What was important was to slow them down so that they could reach the shelter of the wood. Steadying himself as best he could, he took aim. Suddenly the horse sprang over a low boulder and the jolt made him fire. There was a distinct howl of pain from their pursuers and Otto saw one of the leading Cossacks slip with dramatic slowness from his mount, left leg still caught up in his stirrup. Now the man was bouncing along, dragged cruelly behind his mount in a cloud of dust, forcing the riders behind to rein in abruptly or slip to left and right with dextrous movements of their harness in order not to trample him. The wounded Cossack was screaming piteously now as the stones ripped away his flesh.

'We're going to make it, Count!' Otto yelled in triumph, seeing his pursuers drop behind. 'The wood's—'

The words died on his lips. Off to the right, just to the front of the wood, there was a small group of horsemen. Otto didn't need a crystal ball to know who they were – the Cossacks who had slipped off to outflank them. The Count saw them at almost the same moment. Already they were racing towards the two of them, their wild, bearded faces crazed with triumph.

'What can we do, Otto?' he screamed.

'*Pray!*'

The next instant the two groups clashed, the Cossacks yelling furiously. A hand clutched at Otto's reins. His clubbed-pistol smashed down. A tremendous scream – and a Cossack went reeling backwards, flung out of his saddle by the shock of the unexpected blow. A silver sabre blade hissed through the air. Otto's horse reared up on its hind legs, shrieking with pain as a great pink wound suddenly opened on its flank, its hooves flailing the air furiously. Otto reversed his pistol and fired blindly. A Cossack's hands flew to his forehead, bright red blood seeping through his clenched fingers, and he disappeared into a mad welter of swirling dust and flying hooves.

'*Otto*—' Suddenly the Count was gone, his lathered mount sliding forward on its forelegs like a crazy equine skier, to crash into a boulder and come to a sudden halt, blood seeping from its wildly distended nostrils.

'Count!' Otto yelled, urging his horse forward. The older man lay motionless on the ground, two or three Cossack riders rearing above his inert form on their sweating horses. 'I'm coming—'

In absolute rage and panic, he swung his pistol left and right, nearly overbalancing more than once, fighting his way to where his old friend lay. On every side the air was full of howls and curses. Someone grabbed at his leg. He lunged out with his foot. A scream, and a Cossack went staggering back. Another rider collided into him and his horse shuddered under the impact. For one awful moment Otto thought the old nag was going to keel over on the spot. Still it kept going. Now the Count was only a matter of metres away. To left and right the wolfish, cruel faces screamed at him, but he seemed to bear a charmed life: nothing could stop him. A big cross-eyed fellow swung his sabre at him and more by instinct than anything, Otto flung his empty pistol at his face. The man's hooked nose smashed under the impact and he flew backwards over the edge of the high saddle to disappear under the flailing hooves of his comrades' horses.

Then it happened.

Something very hard (later he would discover it was the silver pommel of one of the Cossacks' sabres) struck him over the back of the head. It seemed as if his very brains were shaken loose. He heard someone howling, long, low and mournful like a lonely dog keening at the moon; then he was slipping, slipping, slipping, the wet reins sliding easily from his sweaty hands. All was very peaceful, very slow, very painless. He hit the deck with a sharp grunt. Next instant he was out like a light . . .

EIGHT

'*Ko-lo-ssal!*'

Otto opened his eyes with a groan, closed them again quickly and then opened them once more, but this time not so wide. An enormous woman towered over him on the bed; her white doctor's coat looked as if it had been filled out with a bed-bolster, while her tight skirt bulged and rippled with heavy muscular thighs. Could a woman be that big? he asked himself.

'*Kolossal!*' The enormous woman breathed the German word once more, beaming down at him with a mouthful of stainless steel teeth, undisguised admiration in her eyes.

Otto followed the direction of her gaze and blushed, something he did only on very rare occasions; her gaze was fixed greedily on his loins. Hastily he grabbed for a blanket and pulled it up above his naked body, feeling the soreness and pain at the back of his skull for the first time.

'*Boshe-moi!*' the woman went on. 'You Fritzes have always been blessed by nature.' She rubbed her eyes, as if overcome by emotion. 'We poor Russian women are not used to such luxuries as that.'

'Where am I?' Otto asked hoarsely, looking round at the bare room. The only decoration seemed to be a picture of Stalin above the door and on the nearside white-washed wall, stained with the red splotches of dead bugs, a frighteningly graphic representation of what happened to the male organ during the varying stages of syphilis.

'Romanov Eighth Military Hospital.'

'Military Hospital?' Otto echoed, puzzled, and then felt his head. It was heavily bandaged.

Hurriedly she pulled away his hand. 'Those brutes of Cossacks mishandled you cruelly, my dear Otto,' she said, stroking his hand with an enormous paw twice the size of his own. 'But am I forgetting my courtesies, am I not?' she added very formally. 'You Germans pay great attention to such things. My name is Lemontova, Olga, senior doctor and colonel, second-class,' she snapped, in an impressive *basso profondo*. 'Call me Olga.'

A little overwhelmed by the tremendous woman, who now pressed his hand once again and gave a sigh of infinite longing, her enormous breasts heaving, Otto said in a very weak voice, 'What happened? And where is the Count, er, my companion . . . er, Olga?'

'The Cossacks brought you, the pigs,' she replied, her pudding-like face flushing angrily. 'Said something about you being spies. But the Cossacks have always had spies on the brains.'

'On the *brain*,' Otto corrected her automatically.

'*Spasiba*, Otto,' she said and patted his hand again. 'I am indeed an ignorant woman. I must learn all the time.'

'And my friend?' Otto asked hurriedly.

'The aristocrat?'

'Yes.'

'He was not so hurt as you. He is next door. The Cossacks have placed a guard on him until the—' She stopped short, her brow suddenly furrowed with worry. 'But do not worry, Otto, I, *your* Olga, will look after you. Now I must go. I have patients to attend to, the pigs.' She rose from the edge of the bed. The springs gave a grateful squeak, and with that she was gone, leaving Otto staring at the closed door, wondering what kind of a mess he had got himself into this time.

His mother, the Witch, who often boasted in her cups that she had danced the mattress polka with Napoleon himself when he had come to Berlin in 1809, always maintained that 'gash thinks with what it's got between its legs'. And most times she had been proved right. But as he lay there on the bed listening to the little morning sounds outside, Otto couldn't help wondering how far this particular gash would go to save him and the Count from the NKVD. One thing was for sure; unless they did something, it wouldn't be long before the two of them landed up in the hands of the dreaded Russian Secret Police.

'*Otto*.' A whisper woke him from an uneasy doze. 'Otto, my boy, can you hear me?'

It was the Count, but from where was he speaking? Then he located the source of the sound. It was coming from a chipped, very dirty sink in the corner, under which stood an equally chipped and equally dirty chamber-pot.

Otto raised himself as quickly as he could from his bed and hurried to the sink. Wrinkling his nostrils at the stink, he bent right into it. 'Count, I can hear you. You talking from the basin, too?'

'Yes, it's an old trick I picked up during my days with the Abwehr[1]. It—'

'Don't give me your life story, please,' Otto cut him short. 'We're up to our hooters in crap. This is no time for chats about the past. What do you know?'

'Not a great deal, Otto, save that we are in grave danger.'

'So what else is new? Listen, have you met the woman – the Russian doctor with tits like barrage balloons?'

'Yes. Enormous, isn't she? From what she says and the odd bits of chatter I can make out from the Cossacks outside, she seems to have taken quite a shine to you.' He hesitated, and as Otto waited he saw an ugly black beetle step from behind the tap, stare at him as if mildly surprised to find him there and then scuttle back to cover once more. 'It might be our only chance, Otto.'

'How do you mean?'

'Women are emotional creatures. They'll do a great deal if they are in love.'

[2] The German Secret Service.

'*In love?*' Otto gasped. 'Count, you can't have all your cups in the cupboard! I'd need the fire brigade's biggest ladder just to mount her! No, Count, you can't expect me to do *that!*'

Patiently the invisible Count waited until Otto had finished his tirade, then he said gently, 'All you need to do is to pat her hand and roll your eyes at her and make cooing noises—'

'Pat her hand and make cooing noises!' Otto exploded once more. 'You should have seen the way she looked at my salami a little while back. A piece of gash that size won't be satisfied with hand-patting. She'll want the whole works – and I tell you, I'm scared!'

'Otto, listen to me. We haven't got much time. All we need is our clothing, or some sort of clothing; in my case we'll have to get that Cossack chap guarding the door out of the way. Then we can make a bolt for it.' There was a note of urgent pleading in the Count's voice now. 'That woman is the only way we can do it. She's our last chance, Otto, our very last chance . . . And think of those guns at Miropol.'

Otto swallowed. 'All right, I'll try. But Great God, Count, I don't think I'll survive!' he moaned. 'The things I do for Germany . . .'

'Out of the question, Comrade Colonel,' Doctor Olga was saying at that moment, not fifty metres from a worried young Otto. 'Neither of the – er – prisoners can be moved at the moment, without serious damage to their health.'

'Damage to their health!' Todleben exploded at the other end of the phone. 'Once I've got my hands on the fascist pigs and wrung out the information I need, I shall damage their health – for good!'

Olga thought of the handsome young body she had just seen in all its delightful nakedness only minutes before, and shivered at the thought, but managed to catch herself in time. She resumed her brisk professional manner: 'In due course, the comrades of the NKVD can do with them as they wish. But for the time being they are in my charge, Comrade Colonel – and my decision is that they cannot be moved yet.'

'But they are murderers, killers, spies!' Todleben gave up. 'All right, how long, comrade?'

'Forty-eight hours.'

'So long! *Horoscho*, so be it, but ensure that they are well guarded until I send Major Petrov to take charge. I want them under supervision every minute of the day – they are dangerous resourceful men.'

'Never fear, Comrade, I am well aware of my duties as a loyal communist and member of the Soviet community.' Olga smiled to herself, studying her broad slavic face in the mirror opposite knowingly. 'I shall ensure that they are not left alone for one single moment from now on. I am a patriot, comrade.'

Todleben grunted something inaudible and hung up, leaving Olga alone with her thoughts, which were hot and delightful – and not in the least bit patriotic . . .

'Tests,' she said, patting Otto's hand and looking down at him on the bed like a cow in milk.

'Tests?'

'Yes – just to see if everything is all right.

'But they've just rebandaged my head,' he protested, looking in alarm at the heavy-set nurse in baste slippers; she seemed to be preparing a large needle by blowing down the hollow centre-piece, completing the operation by wiping the point on the back of her apron.

'It is not your head I am examining, my dear Otto,' Olga said. With a sudden swift movement she whipped down the blanket, to reveal his nakedness.

'Hey!' Otto cried, but it was too late; Olga had already taken out a spatula of the kind used by doctors in

Germany to examine throats, and gently placing it under
his member, raised it thus. For a while she examined it
with professional curiosity – though her soft sighs and the
rather hectic heaving of her massive bosom indicated that
her motives were not altogether professional. Finally she
nodded and murmured, '*Horoscho* – good, very good. Not
a pimple anywhere.' She turned to the hefty nurse with the
needle and said something in Russian.

Suddenly the woman reached forward and grabbed Otto.
Before he knew what was happening, she had thrown him
on his face, slapped his left buttock and rammed home the
long needle, holding him effortlessly with one hand while
she completed the operation, smiling as he screeched with
pain.

Finally the torture was over, and Otto was glowering up
at the two grinning women, his face red with shame and
anger. 'And what was all that about, then?' he demanded.

'Some elementary precautions, my dearest Otto,' Olga
said, soothing his arm with a hand like a small steam-
shovel. 'I don't think the Wassermann is necessary.' She
beamed lovingly at him.

'Precautions? *Wassermann?*' he stuttered. 'What in three
devils' name *is* all this?'

'We're going to have a party tonight, a real Russian party
in your honour, Otto.' Suddenly her normal bass voice
gave way to a girlish, virginal simper. 'And one never
knows what happens at parties, does one?' She lowered
her great pudding-face as if overcome by shyness, and
whispered, 'Especially if one is young – and romantic!'

Five minutes later, Otto's head was bent over the dirty,
smelly wash-basin as he told the Count his startling news;
he also informed him that he would ensure that he, the
Count, was invited to the party – or there would be no
party. In return he listened while the Count warned him
about the Russian addiction to alcohol – he would have to

keep his own drinking to a minimum if they were going to use this 'God-given opportunity' to escape.

'Don't worry yourself there, Count,' Otto answered warily. 'I'm keeping the old wooden eye wide open this particular night. Otherwise that Popov Olga'll have the knickers off me as quick as lightning—'

Suddenly he jumped up with a yell, banging his head on the tap. The other Russian woman had come in and caught him bending provocatively over the sink, naked as he was. Obviously she hadn't been able to resist the temptation. Now she grinned at him good-humouredly. 'In Russia, we sick *after* the party,' she said, indicating the sink. 'German – he different, yes?'

'Yes, German, he different, yes,' Otto said sourly, rubbing his bandaged head. 'And you keep your hands to yourself next time. You Russkis must be a sex-starved bunch, that's all I can say.' And with that he limped back to his bed, followed by her admiring gaze.

NINE

'*Musika! Vodka! Kleba!*' Olga cried in Russian. Her straw-coloured blonde hair was loosened from the tight braids now, and her enormous frame clad in a kind of taffeta bell-tent beneath which her loose flesh rippled, as if caught in a great wind, every time she clapped her hands.

Men and women came rushing into the room. The women, perhaps nurses in the Eighth Field Hospital, but all big and busty, were bearing dishes laden with cold meats, gherkins in sour cream, heaped piles of dark brown bread, sprinkled with caraway seed. The men bore one thing only – vodka.

The drink started to flow. In the corner of the crowded, steamy hospital room, a little cross-eyed man started to play the accordion. A great tumbler of vodka was thrust into Otto's hand and Olga, looking down at his bewildered young face, slapped him hard on the back and cried: 'Drink, little Otto! *Nastrovya pan!*'

As he took a deep draught, the back of his skull seemed to explode. Now there were men and women thrusting drinks at him from all sides. Drinks in glasses, drinks in bottles, even drinks in the chamber-pot. The room began to whirl.

The Cossacks threw down their weapons and joined in the carousing, their prisoners forgotten now. The Count staggered in, as drunk as the rest, his face unwashed and covered with two days' growth of beard. He smiled a little helplessly over the heads of the excited mob of men and women. 'The Russian soul!' he shouted, as if that explained the total uproar. Moments later Otto saw him trying to dance Russian-style on the floor, arms linked with two of the Cossacks. Then he disappeared from view.

'The Americans can everything,' Otto heard someone say in German to his right, but he was pressed up too tight to Olga's massive bosom to be able to turn to the speaker. 'Their Army runs on canned goods. They even say they can cunt for the soldiers!'

Standing on the table, kicking bottles to left and right, a Cossack began to dance, a dagger between his teeth and twirling two glittering sabres very dangerously with his hands. For some reason his trousers were around his ankles – revealing the truth of the rumour that Cossacks do not wear underpants.

'*Cossacks!*' Olga roared, and flinging up the bell-tent in the dancing Cossack's direction, exposed a great yellow moon of bare flesh. Shocked, the Cossack fell off the table. His comrades, their dark eyes wild with excitement under their rakish fur caps, thrust their fingers in between their teeth and shrilled fierce whistles of approval.

Olga took up the challenge. With surprising agility for such an enormous woman, she sprang on the table vacated by the Cossack. It groaned frantically under her weight, but didn't collapse – yet. As the Cossacks clapped fervently, making the same whistling sounds they used to urge on their mounts, she crossed her plump arms above her massive purple bosom and began to kick out her muscular legs with great determination, the sweat pouring down her pudding-face in huge rivulets.

'Take the knout to her,' the man who had spoken German said. He was a little fellow with a mouthful of blackened teeth and one eye missing. 'That's the only thing a Russian woman understands. The knout. They love you more afterwards.'

'But what is a knout?' Otto asked drunkenly, gaping in open-mouthed wonder at the mountains of naked white flesh that Olga was now displaying.

He never did find out. Next moment the table collapsed. Olga's steel teeth flew from her mouth and she flopped down on the swimming floor with a tremendous crash.

Enflamed by the sight of all that naked white flesh, a bearded Cossack seized his opportunity and thrust a hand up Olga's skirt, as she squatted there, legs wide apart on the floor. Olga didn't hesitate. Drawing back a ham-like fist, she launched a tremendous blow at the Cossack's chin. The punch sent him skidding across the floor to crash into the cross-eyed accordion player, who let out a sudden improvised ripple of notes at the impact and then slumped unconscious over the inert body of the Cossack.

'I was named after the German princesses – Anna, Olga, Dora!' Olga roared, and staggered drunkenly to her feet. 'Can't let a common Cossack feel *my* thing!' She grabbed at the brimming chamber-pot of vodka which was being circulated close by and took a tremendous slug of it.

'My wife had jugs like that.' The sour-faced German-speaker loomed up out of the fog that now seemed to have settled down permanently in front of Otto's eyes. 'Jugs this big!' He thrust out his dirty little paws, as if he were holding on to an enormous rucksack. 'When she was wearing a bra, you couldn't get close enough to her to stick in yer piece of salami!' He mimed a woman undoing the catch of her brassiere and giving a sigh of relief. 'Only time you could get close to her was when she let 'em flop. In God's name, wasn't she proud of those jugs of hers! Flaunt 'em, she would. Stick 'em under men's noses, as if she were offering 'em for a bit of suck on a silver platter. But I showed her. I—'

Otto never heard the sour little man's account of how he tamed his wife, for just in that instant an empty bottle tossed to one side by one of the drunken Cossacks struck the man on the side of the head and he went out like a light, joining the others who were now beginning to litter the soaked floor on all sides.

The vodka continued to flow.

Otto had a confused, blurred picture of a tall officer with the green cross of the NKVD on his cap entering the room. He appeared, or so Otto thought, to protest at the party. But after the first deep gulp from the chamber-pot, his hat seemed to slip somehow down on one side. His face flushed red. A little while later his tunic was ripped wide open and he was attempting to play *Deutschland über Alles* on the accordion, while half a dozen Cossacks tried, but failed, to stand to attention. Otto lost sight of him after that. Still the vodka flowed in torrents.

Now Otto was slumped on the edge of a wooden bench, on which lay a drunken Cossack, face downwards, hands tightly clutching the sides as if he was afraid he might fall off at any moment like a man in a small boat in a high sea. A great wench of a nurse was trying to feed him a dung-coloured nipple as big as a plum, in an apparent attempt to revive him. Otto watched in open-mouthed incomprehension.

Now more and more of the heavy-set nurses began to rip off their clothes. The Count made a brief appearance, rising from the floor and crying, 'Ladies, ladies, where is the well-known Russian *kultura*? *Ich bitte Sie!*'

'*Nix kultura!*' The nurse who had grabbed Otto's eggs stumbled forward, dragging down her knee-length, bright green issue drawers eagerly as she did so. '*Kultura* between my legs!' Gleefully she jumped on top of the prostrate Count, who disappeared from sight once more. Otto looked away as swiftly as he could manage – it was a dreadful sight. And the vodka continued to flow.

Thus Otto and the Russians caroused on the night of June 21st, 1941, while the events which would change all their lives, and indeed the history of the world for the rest of the twentieth century ran their inevitable course not more than a hundred kilometres away.

On that long frontier with Russia, the historic moment had come. Everywhere silent processions of infantry had risen and started to take their positions for the great attack, their faces solemn, fervent with hope. Now a vast loneliness overcame them as they stared up at that immense velvet sky, these young men who would soon kill and be killed; it was as if they were living suspended between two planets. For there were none so insensitive among them who did not know that the dawn would change their lives for good. They would never be the same again.

As they lay there in the damp fields of corn, or crouched in the cover of the resin-heavy woods, listening to their heartbeats and feeling their lungs inhale and exhale the precious breath, counting off the minutes to 'X-hour', the generals and the politicians in their starched uniforms and well-pressed suits studied their maps, read their last-minute reports, prepared to match their moral strength and intellectual ingenuity against as yet unknown opponents. *Would their gamble pay off?*

Now it was exactly two hours to the start of Operation Barbarossa. From the Black Sea in the south to Finland in the north, the millions of young men waited . . .

But in that remote hospital, which would soon be packed with desperately wounded and dying men, the vodka flowed and pleasure was uppermost in the minds of those who were still conscious.

'Otto!' Olga breathed, swaying wildly from side to side as she towered above him on the bench, next to the sea-sick Cossack and the nurse trying to revive him with her nipple. Otto cowered back, unable to run. Somewhere or other she had lost her stainless steel teeth. Now she gave him a fumbling, wet kiss and started to sing in a deep bass, imitating the popular Swedish singer Zarah Leander and reeling from side to side as if she were in the grip of a gale: '*Der Wind hat mir ein Lied erzählt . . . das was schön . . . Er weiss was . . .*' Then, fixing him with an hypnotic look of love, she started to take off the taffeta bell-tent, still singing drunkenly.

Otto blanched. 'No – *no!*' he croaked. Wildly he summoned up his feeble reserves of Russian, thinking that it might penetrate her intoxicated reverie as she drew the bell-tent over her head to reveal her enormous whale-like body: '*Nyet . . . nyet . . . pashalstya . . .* I'm not well.'

He pressed his back against the wall, eyes wild and wide with terror as she advanced upon him, totally naked now, making little wet kissing noises with her toothless gums. '*Help!*' he cried. '*Help!*'

But there was no help forthcoming this June dawn. Suddenly her two great dugs were thrust into his face and his last scream was muffled in an avalanche of soft flesh. The bench collapsed beneath them. Otto fell on his back, and Olga, clutching him as if her life depended on it, fell on top of him. Her weight knocked all remaining fight out of him. With a little squeak of sheer delight, she went to work upon him. Otto, defeated at last, let it happen . . .

'Otto, my boy, do you live?'

Otto heard the Count's whispered comment as if from a million kilometres away. His eyes remained firmly screwed shut. 'No, I've been dead for hours.'

'Take a drink of this,' the Count whispered. 'It's water,' he added hastily, realizing by Otto's groan that he thought it might be more alcohol.

Eyes still pressed close, Otto gratefully accepted the drink, letting it trickle down his parched throat, quenching what seemed to be a Sahara Desert of a thirst. Finally he had had enough. He croaked, 'I daren't open my eyes to check, Count, but could you have a look?' There was a note of pleading in his voice. 'Is . . . is it still . . . there?'

The Count patted his arm reassuringly. 'Of course, it is, my boy, though it is . . . er . . . slightly damaged.'

Otto breathed out a sigh of relief. 'Mary, Joseph, Jesus, thank Christ!' He opened his eyes.

There were drunken snoring Russians everywhere, most of them naked. A metre or so away, Olga's mountainous rump rose into the air like the North Face of the Eiger. She was snoring mightily like a knackered old steam bellows, a beatific look on her pudding-face. The sight of Olga reminded him of something else. He flashed a look at his naked loins. 'Shit on the shingle – she's stolen it!' he gasped.

The Count patted him. 'You have paid a terrible price for our freedom, I must admit, but it was worth it – and there'll be a gong in it for you, I'm sure.'

'It's not a gong, I want,' Otto snarled. 'It's a *new dong*!'

With that, he let himself be hauled to his feet by the Count, and while the Russians slept, they tip-toed around, looking for suitable gear among the huge piles of hastily abandoned clothing. Otto crossed over to the snoring NKVD officer, concertina still clasped to his naked chest and resting on the head of a nurse who had fallen asleep in an act of mild perversion, and gently removed the pistol from his holster. 'You never know,' he said.

The Count nodded. Gingerly, very gingerly, they began to creep towards the door – and freedom.

Suddenly they froze. Olga had risen like some great white hippo, eyes firmly screwed shut, bosom heaving as if she were still deep asleep. 'Kiss me, Otto,' she commanded in a deep bass.

Otto looked at the Count. The Count looked back, almost in awe. 'What a people,' he whispered. 'Never can they get enough!' Then he dug Otto in the ribs. 'Kiss her.'

Otto obeyed mechanically. She sank into sleep once more, snoring pleasurably, and the last Otto ever saw of her as he passed through the door into a new dawn already flushed pink with the silent gunfire of the opening barrage, was that great moon of an arse. It was a sight that would give the handsome young German nightmares for many a year to come.

TEN

'Pig! Lecherous, drink-sodden pig!' Todleben snarled, and lashing out with his knout, curled the black whip around Petrov's naked shoulders as he slumped there dejectedly in the hospital's cobbled courtyard.

Petrov howled with pain, yelling something in a tongue that Todleben could not understand; but the Cossacks of the firing squad obviously could. For in spite of their tremendous hangovers, their dark, savage eyes gleamed with sudden awareness.

Up above on the third floor, Olga, a vinegar-soaked bandage wrapped around her head, her face very pale and with dark circles under her eyes, was half-listening to comrade Stalin's thick Georgian voice booming out over the loudspeaker fixed above the door at the far end of the corridor.

'The entire Soviet people is rising in defence of the Fatherland at the side of the Red Army,' he was saying. 'It is a question of life and death for the Soviet State, for the people of the USSR – a question whether the peoples of the Soviet Union shall be free or reduced to slavery.'

Olga approved one hundred per cent of comrade Stalin's sentiments; but at this particular moment she was too hungover and miserable at the loss of her German lover to be able to conjure up the right kind of enthusiasm for the war which had been sprung upon the Soviet Fatherland so treacherously.

'Great Lenin, who founded our State, used to say that the basic qualities of Soviet men should be valour and daring,' Stalin droned on, while below Todleben thrashed the helpless NKVD officer with his whip, heedless of the glowering looks of the still drunken Cossacks. 'They should be fearless in battle and resolved to fight against the enemies of our country. The Red Army and Navy and all the citizens of the Soviet Union must defend every inch of the Soviet soil, fight to the last drop of their blood, defend their towns and villages and show their daring and ingenuity – qualities that are characteristic of our people.'

Across in the little town, the sirens started to emit their stomach-churning wail. Old women and children, herding chickens and pigs in front of them in the dusty streets, hurried to the earthen shelters. Middle-aged men in helmets, wearing new armbands on their sleeves, ran up and down, shouting and waving rattles.

Olga held her aching temples. What did it mean? she asked herself, and took another cooling sip of beer from the great two-litre bottle on the window ledge.

Below, Todleben seemed not to hear the sirens. He continued to lash Petrov's naked upper body with his cruel, many-thonged whip, sending him reeling back and forth across the courtyard until he was gasping for breath and red-faced with exertion. Only then did he cease. His chest heaving in his elegant uniform, now stained black with sweat, he turned to the Cossack officer. '*Sotnik*,' he commanded, 'shoot the treacherous pig – shoot him down like an animal, this instant!'

As the sirens ceased their howling a heavy expectant silence descended upon the yard, broken only by the drone of Stalin's voice: 'In this war of liberation, we shall not be alone. We shall have faithful allies in the peoples of Europe and America. Our war for the freedom of the Fatherland is merged into the struggle of the peoples of Europe and America for their independence and freedom. It is the united front of the peoples who stand for freedom against the threat of enslavement by Hitler's fascist armies.'

'*Sotnik*,' Todleben cried petulantly, 'we have no time to waste! What are you waiting for?' Reaching into his pocket,

Todleben took out one of the caramels that he always gave
to the pretty boys, unwrapped it and popped it into his
sore mouth. Petrov looked up at the Cossack Captain
imploringly. From far off there came the sound of many
planes. At her window, Olga looked up slowly. The
morning sky was an endless blue, pristine and empty. She
ignored the noise.

Down below, the *Sotnik*, his sabre gleaming silver in the
slanting rays of the sun, swung round and barked a hoarse
command. The Cossacks clicked to attention. Todleben,
sucking his sweet, flung a contemptuous glance at the
wretched Petrov and stepped hastily out of the way.

'Load . . . aim!' the *Sotnik* cried crisply.

The firing squad brought up their weapons.

The noise of planes was growing louder. But all the
participants were too engrossed in the scene taking place
before their eyes to pay any attention to it.

'Squad!' the Sotnik barked, and raised his sabre,
'Squad—'

There was a sudden howl. Everyone flung a glance
upwards. Above Romanov, four sinister black shades
hovered almost motionless in the still blue sky. There was
something terrifying in their effortless hovering. The
Sotnik froze there, sabre upraised.

Todleben spat out the sweet. 'Get on with it, man!' he
cried, suddenly enraged. 'Or do you want me to use the
knout on *you* too?'

Suddenly the leading plane waggled its gull-like wings,
and fell from the sky. There was a tremendous, spine-
chilling howl as it plummeted earthwards at an incredible
speed, siren screaming.

'*Air raid!*' Olga screamed and dropped her bandage.

'In this connection,' Stalin was saying, 'the historic
utterance of the British Prime Minister Mr Churchill about
aid to the Soviet Union—'

Just as the Stuka seemed about to crash into the ground,

its pilot levelled out and a rain of tiny black bombs came hurtling out of its evil blue belly.

'Comrades,' Stalin cried, 'our forces are numberless. The overweening enemy will soon learn this to his cost. Side by side with the Red Army many thousand workers, collective farmers—'

The appeal was drowned by the detonation of the bombs. In Romanov a whole line of peasant cottages was directly hit. As their straw roofs burst into flame, civilians ran out into the streets screaming. Immediately a great mushroom of smoke started to rise into the still blue sky.

Olga grabbed hold of the windowsill as the next Stuka came howling out of the sky, hurtling down at four hundred kilometres an hour, its screaming sirens turning her blood to water.

'The Russian people will rise in their millions,' Stalin exhorted, as the Stuka flattened out of its tremendous, death-defying dive. Again the bombs came tumbling down, exploding with the roar of an infuriated beast. As flames burst out all around him, Todleben became aware of his own danger; the ground shook and quaked under his feet and dislodged tiles were now beginning to tumble from the hospital's roof into the courtyard. '*Finish him off!*' he cried above the howl of the diving Stukas. '*Shoot the treacherous bastard!*'

Beside himself with rage, Todleben savagely swung his knout at the *Sotnik*, who staggered back with a howl of pain, a sudden fig-red, gleaming slash across his pale cheek.

Petrov staggered to his feet. 'Brothers, Cossacks,' he cried with new strength, pointing to the gull-like planes overhead, 'the day of liberation has come! We Cossacks of the Don can be free once again!'

'So *that's* it!' Olga breathed to herself, watching the tense scene below, realizing that Petrov was a Don Cossack, one of that tribe which fought the Red Army right into the twenties, long after the rest of the White resistance had been broken.

'Comrades!' Petrov cried again, his arms spread out wide as if he wished to embrace his executioners. 'Raise the black flag of our poor people once more!'

'Treachery! On all sides, treachery!' Todleben bellowed, his handsome face flushed crimson with rage. Dropping his knout, he grabbed for his revolver, but too late – in the same instant the *Sotnik* whom he had struck with the whip ran straight at him, his sabre flashing silver in the sun. Todleben gave one last terrible scream as the keen blade clove his skull in two and a rich, red pulp spurted up from his head. The pistol dropped weakly from his lifeless fingers. But still he remained on his feet.

The fact seemed to enrage the *Sotnik* even more. He raised the sabre, its silver blade now flushed crimson with blood, and slashed it down one final time. Todleben's head flew into the dust, leaving the rump squatting there as if forever.

'The tyrant is dead!' Petrov screamed hysterically, as the firing squad broke and started plunging their bayonets with atavastic primeval fury into the headless corpse.

'*The tyrant is dead!*' the Cossacks took up the wild cry. '*Kill the Jews! Kill the money-bags! Death to the commissars!*' Now they were streaming out of the courtyard, waving their weapons, intent on rape and loot and murder just like their primitive forefathers in times gone by.

Olga took a last look at Todleben's face, set in a hideous snarl of death, blood and pink-tinged spittle still bubbling out from between clenched teeth; then, as the air-raid sirens began to wail the all-clear, she started to bellow out orders to the frightened nurses and orderlies crouched at the far end of the corridor. 'Hand out rifles to the orderlies! You sisters, buckle on your duty pistols while you're working! Put a guard on the medical alcohol! Lock the doors to the ward and keep the windows barred! I want guards in the kitchens and pantries to prevent looting!'

Olga had been through all this before in 1917, when as a teen-aged girl, she had witnessed the outbreak of the Revolution. She had been raped twice, starved most of the time and once been machine-gunned by a White armoured train. She knew what to expect now.

'*Well?*' she cried in exasperation, seeing that her subordinates hadn't moved. 'Don't you understand?' Her eyes blazed from her pudding-face with sudden fury at their tardiness and stupidity. 'It's not just a war we're going to have to fight – it's a breakdown of the Soviet State! By the Black Virgin of Kazan – *move! This is the revolution . . . !*'

BOOK TWO: THE BATTLE FOR MIROPOL

'Up came a spider, sat down beside her, whipped his old bazooka out and this is what he said . . .'

British Soldier's Dirty Ditty, W.W.II.

ONE

It was clear right from the start of the great operation that the Russians had been taken completely by surprise. Almost at once, the German Signals Intercept Service listening to Russian communications to their immediate front picked up a confused, panic-stricken signal: 'We are being attacked,' it read. 'What shall we do?' The answer from senior headquarters was: 'You must be crazy! Why should the Germans attack us? And why wasn't your signal in code?'

On that burning hot day of June 1941, it was the same story everywhere. Great hauls of prisoners, thousands of them, were made all along the front. In great, smelly brown columns they marched past the waiting tank crews to the rear, giving off the foul stench of a monkey-house in some ill-kept provincial zoo, only too happy to be out of it all and smiling at the tankers waiting to go into action as if they were friends, not enemies.

The mutinies started almost at once. At Brest-Litovsk, the Ukrainians of the 2nd Infantry Division mutinied, attempted to kill their commanders and political commissars and surrender to the Germans. Those who managed to break through, chased by the machine-gun bullets of loyal regiments, kissed the German invaders' boots and welcomed them as liberators.

As the Germans marched into the dusty villages of the Ukraine, they were astonished to be greeted not by bullets, but by smiling, grateful village headmen, bearing the traditional gifts of friendship and welcome – freshly-baked bread, salt, and vodka. For a while yet they would be regarded as liberators. Meanwhile in Moscow, Beria, the head of the NKVD, ordered that the peasant reservists being assembled in the capital to meet the advancing Germans should be given a ration of two litres of vodka, locked up in their barracks under the guard of his NKVD troops, and then marched to the front. Chaos, breakdown, and treachery were in the air everywhere.

Now the first waves of infantry began the long pursuit of the fleeing remnants of the broken Frontier Army; slogging through the burning dust, their grey faces wet with sweat, they tossed all unnecessary equipment aside, so that their progress was marked by lines of abandoned gas-masks, greatcoats and spare boots. Hour after hour they marched ever eastwards through the blinding dust and burning heat, singing the same old marching songs, eating up the kilometres of that limitless steppe. They were exhausted but triumphant, for now there was victory in the air. Soon their task would be over, and then it would be the turn of the tanks to plunge right into the heart of the dying Soviet Union. Soon Adolf Hitler's own élite Bodyguard Division would go into action – and that would be the end for the Popovs.

The blond giants of the Bodyguard waited impatiently in their laagers in fields and orchards. The air around them was heavy with the smell of lush grass, but tinged every now and again with a whiff of acrid smoke from the heavy guns pounding the fleeing enemy twenty kilometres away.

Angrily, General Dietrich paced up and down in the dust. Was von Manstein going to leave him out of the war altogether? In the distance he could hear the permanent heavy barrage beginning to recede. With it, as Dietrich knew, went the battle too, watched by his dismayed officers, who saw their decorations vanish with the thunder of the artillery. *When would they be employed?*

The call to action came finally, not with a blast from a

THE MIROPOL POSITION, JUNE 1941.

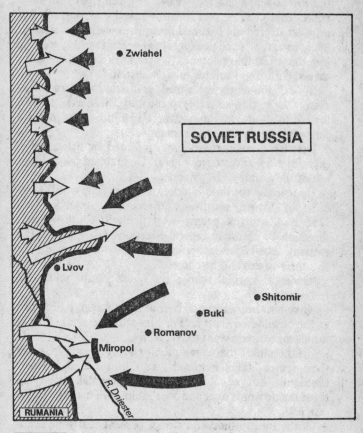

SOVIET RUSSIA

● Zwiahel

● Shitomir

● Buki

● Romanov

Lvov

Miropol

R. Dniester

RUMANIA

 = German Attacks

 = Russian Counter-attacks

 = German Occupied Terrritory

trumpet or the crackle of excited morse over the air waves, but in the shape of a fat, weary, dispatch-rider clad in an ankle-length leather coat, his face caked with dust. Grumpily, he steered his battered machine towards the straggle of command cars and pausing at the nearest sentry, growled in a thick Hamburg accent, 'Where's yer Old Man? Got a message for him from his nibs, Manstein.'

'*What!*' the sentry exclaimed, spinning round and completely forgetting all military courtesy. 'General,' he bellowed, 'it's – it . . . I mean, there's an important message for you from the Army Commander.'

Dietrich came at the double, followed by half a dozen eager blond giants. 'Give it here.' He grabbed the message out of the grumpy DR's hands.

He scanned the lines rapidly, muttering the words as he did so; 'Move north-east direction . . . Olyka and Dubno . . . attack enemy west flank in south-westerly direction . . . Head in general direction of Rovno . . .' His swarthy face broke into a great gold-toothed smile. 'It's the order to march!' he chortled.

'Order to march!' echoed the blond giants, taking up the cry.

'Give him beer, as much beer as he can drink,' he yelled at the bewildered sentry. 'Fill him with the stuff. Pour it up his arse, if you want to. *We march!*'

On the tanks, the young men, who were soon to die in their scores, their hundreds, and in the end in their thousands, hugged and embraced in sheer delight, crying those magic words over and over again. 'We march . . . *We march!*'

Of the twenty thousand troops present that June evening, only two hundred would survive.

Luck! A head-on assault, carried through with reckless courage and taken at the double. The cost: half-tracks, armoured cars, self-propelled guns, tanks blackened with fire, tipped on their sides, burning fiercely, their crews scattered in the churned earth around them in a bloody circle, like a pile of chopped meat-waste from a butcher's shop.

Dubno! Infantry attack. The steppe littered with the big corpses of the panzer grenadiers in their camouflaged smocks, sack-like and stiff, a patch of black blood in their ears, a brown stain at the corner of their mouths, a curl of hardening pink at their pinched nostrils, and always their fists clenched, as if angry at the cruel trick fate had played on them in their moment of victory.

Olyka! A mess of hopeless rubble and ruins, houses cut in two revealing the pathetic intimacies of peasant life, iron girders snapped like matchsticks, the labour of centuries destroyed in a few short hours. And the dead tanks again, the steel beasts of death themselves killed by steel, their turrets decapitated by anti-tank fire, their giant limbs ripped off by mines, their metal flesh gouged by solid shot leaving behind gleaming silver wounds.

On and on, the Bodyguard raced over the endless, burning steppe. Time and time again, the radio crackled in Dietrich's command car and the sweating, unshaven operator would swing round, not even taking the time to remove his earphones, to report yet another success. *Podhorce taken . . . Leiczany fallen . . . Station at Chorlupy in our hands . . . Turczyn about to surrender . . .* It seemed that nothing could stop the steel monster of the German Army as it crawled over that foreign earth, destroying everything in its path.

Bronki! The prisoners came streaming in, an earth-brown crocodile, eight deep, shuffling westwards, herded onwards by mounted chain-dogs, swinging their whips like cowboys on some great cattle-drive of the Old West; miserably, the prisoners would beg for water, ripping stray dogs to pieces with their bare hands and stuffing the raw, bleeding flesh into their mouths greedily before their comrades could steal it from them.

Klevan! The steppe white with propaganda leaflets dropped by the *Luftwaffe*, promising a 'Safe Pass for officers or men up to fifty in number'; Russian stragglers roasting dried pig-dung over wood fires, wasted already to human skeletons with great burning black eyes by the combat of these last terrible days.

Broniki! The infantry hurl themselves against the Russian guns, howling like infuriated beasts. Countless flashes slash the woods to their front. Trees fall like matchsticks. The barrage advances. Still the infantry press onwards, heads bent as if toiling against a great wind. Flames, shrapnel as big as a man's fist, hissing copper driving bands. Now the gaps begin to appear in the ranks of the advancing grenadiers. Now they are through, leaving the dusty plain behind them littered with their great corpses; German soldiers rushing for the squat huts and enemy-held block-houses, seized by a desperate blood-fury, hacking, slashing, gouging, showing no quarter and expecting none, ripping at the terrified men in their baggy pants and earth-coloured blouses with their bare hands, physically tearing them apart.

And so on to the next God-forsaken village, leaving the corpses to be gathered up and piled on horse-drawn carts like stacks of wood; bodies clasping each other in fraternal embrace, grinning with distorted faces; and the burning tanks dotting the plain vomiting ghostly black smoke-rings.

On and on, and ever closer to Miropol.

Miropol – it was a name that was now beginning to haunt an unshaven, shrunken-faced, exhausted General Dietrich. Where were his spies? What awaited him at the Miropol Position?

TWO

They were squatting on the bank at the side of the dusty white ribbon road that led eastwards from Romanov. It was packed, as were all the roads which they had marched along since making their escape two days ago. But they were no longer worried. The mob of deserters and panic-stricken civilians fleeing eastwards before the advancing Germans were too preoccupied with their own safety to take any interest in them. If they looked up at all, it was only to cast a fearful glance at the burning blue sky to check whether the *Luftwaffe* had spotted them. The dive-bombers and straffing fighters of the German Air Force were everywhere these days, ranging far and wide in front of the Army, spreading terror and panic wherever they went.

Otto rubbed his hot, blistered feet. The Cossack boots he wore were too big for him, and his heels were red-raw where the leather had chafed his bare feet. Down below, a group of peasants streamed past, the children herding geese and a lone, skinny-ribbed cow in front of them, while the womenfolk, all hooded like nuns, squatted on a little cart piled high with their pathetic possessions, drawn by an emaciated bullock, whose tongue hung low as if it were at the end of its tether. All sobbed in a quiet, resigned way.

Otto paused in his rubbing. 'Poor peasant shits,' he said, wearily but without emotion, for he had seen countless such sights in these last forty-eight hours. 'I wonder where they think they're running to, eh, Count?'

The Count rubbed his unshaven chin, the stubble

crackling under his dirty fingers. 'I don't know, Otto. But they won't be going far . . .' With a tired gesture he indicated the horizon to the west, which shimmered an ominous, silent pink above the blue ripples of the heat haze. 'The permanent barrage, Otto,' he explained. 'Theirs in this case – so our troops can't be far away now.'

'How far do you estimate?'

Further down the road some sort of guard was herding along a collection of lunatics, grinning with inane smiles as if this was some sort of wonderful excursion. Saliva dribbled from the sides of their slack mouths; snot dripped from their broad noses. Otto looked away hastily.

'Visibility is very good,' the Count said after a moment. 'The Russians could be perhaps thirty kilometres off, so you can reckon our people are thirty-five to forty kilometres away now.' He looked strangely at Otto, but said nothing.

Otto had been with the Count long enough to know all his moods and looks. He said, 'You're thinking of the Miropol Position, aren't you?'

The Count nodded.

'But what can we do? Sneak through the Popov lines, perhaps, and warn Dietrich?'

'I have given it much thought, Otto . . .' The Count seemed to be choosing his words with great care and deliberation; obviously he was leading up to something, and at this moment Otto had a vague suspicion that it would be unpleasant and dangerous. 'But I fear we wouldn't stand much chance of getting through the Russian front. Even if we did, there would still be a distinct possibility that we might be shot by our own people. You recollect from our experiences in Holland in '40 just how trigger-happy soldiers—'

'*Count!*' Otto interrupted him firmly. 'Now just what have you got in mind?'

'We came all this way to discover the strength of the Miropol Position, didn't we? And we discovered that if those great cannon are not put out of action before the

Bodyguard comes within range, the Division will be massacred.'

'If you're thinking what I think you're thinking, you can forget it,' Otto said. Already he felt a cold finger of fear tracing the length of his spine. 'How in Hell's name do you think we could tackle those shitting great pop-guns?' Anger overcame him. 'Even if we could get inside the turrets, we've got no explosives, no means of spiking them, no nothing except one stupid shitting Popov pistol, and if I know the Popovs, I'm willing to bet that doesn't work either!'

The Count seemed unmoved by Otto's sudden outburst. 'But I've been giving it thought, Otto, my dear boy. I've got a plan.'

'*Pl*—' Otto's cry of 'plan' changed suddenly into a fearful '*plane!*' A single-engined fighter had come barrelling in at tree-top height, cannon and machine-guns already chattering, evil blue-and-red lights crackling along its wings. 'Hit the dirt, Count!' Otto screamed frantically.

Panic-stricken, the civilians on the road below scattered. But it was already too late. The Messerschmidt roared along the column, spitting fire. Men, women, children, animals went down on all sides. *Whack . . . Whack* – its cannon thumped away, pumping searing-white 20*mm* shells into the farm carts and old trucks. All around Otto and the Count, the earth erupted. Stone chippings flew in every direction and earth showered down on them as they lay there, hands held tightly over their heads like frightened children. As suddenly as it had appeared, the fighter was zooming off into the brilliant blue sky, rolling over and over in triumph, leaving behind burning vehicles and a litter of dead bodies sprawled out in the extravagant attitudes of the violently done to death.

Otto looked at the Count. 'War,' the latter said, 'it's war, Otto.'

'It's not war,' the younger man snarled, 'it's murder – plain, simple murder! Come on.'

Together they staggered to their feet and began to trudge westwards once more, trying to avoid looking at the old women with leathery, wrinkled faces, kneeling beside their dead. Try as he might to block out the sound of their keening, Otto felt the small hairs at the back of his head prickle with fear. That afternoon there was no more talk of Miropol . . .

Now the whole countryside was a-flutter with white. Every miserable little straw-roofed peasant *isba* was draped with a white tablecloth, sheet or even a towel, to indicate that the inhabitants were ready to surrender. Here and there, as Otto and the Count marched through the hamlets, they saw little knots of silent peasants standing at the wayside looking westwards, as if they half-expected the Germans to appear at any moment. But mostly the cottages and more solidly-built houses of the small towns were tightly shut-tered, their doors nailed up from inside, giving the two lone travellers the eerie feeling that their progress was being watched by scores of fearful eyes peering through the slits in the woodwork.

Just as the sun started to go down and the burning white glare of the day began to give way to the glowing purple of the Russian evening, they came to a bridge over what looked like a canal, and found their way barred by a convoy of horse-drawn artillery, the riders, their lathered mounts and the ancient wooden-wheeled guns all covered in thick, grey dust. Otto and the Count halted and waited for the artillerymen to pass. They knew they had nothing to fear – the look in the eyes of the soldiers told them that. The men looked broken, at the end of their tether, their only concern to get away from whoever or whatever was pursuing them.

As Otto and the Count looked on, a staff car filled with high-ranking officers braked to a stop at the far side of the bridge. Officers poured from it and commenced shouting

at the weary artillerymen. They shouted back. Suddenly
there was a shot, and one of the officers was reeling back,
clutching his chest, a look of utter surprise in his eyes.
Another officer doubled back to the staff car. Reaching in,
he brought out a round-barrelled tommy-gun.

'Duck!' Otto cried hastily.

Just as they hit the cobbles, a wild burst of gunfire from
the officer on the far side of the bridge hissed over their
heads. Artillerymen screamed shrilly and dropped from
their mounts. A horse whinnied piteously and rose up in
its traces, hooves flailing crazily. Panic broke out on all
sides. Now the bridge was a confused mêlée of rearing
horses, reeling gun carriages, firing men, and tracer zipping
back and forth like angry red hornets.

Otto pressed closer to the Count. 'When I give the word,
make a break for the water!' he yelled above the snap and
crackle of the angry fire fight.

'*Water?*'

'Yes – we can't go back now, and there's no going
forward over that bridge. This is going to go on for hours
yet, and where there are staff officers, there's bound to be
bulls. And you know what'll happen when the bulls come
on the scene.'

'What?'

'They'll start shooting anybody who ain't at least a
colonel. Now keep yer head low, Count, and yer arsehole
tight. One . . . two . . . three – *here we go!*'

Otto rose to his feet, and with his head tucked deep
between his shoulders like an American football-player
running a touchdown, he pelted for the water, angry
bullets kicking up little blue flashes of sparks and stones at
his heels.

The Count followed more slowly, zig-zagging crazily,
dodging the bullets by a hair's breadth time and time
again.

Otto skidded to a halt at the top of the muddy bank and
flung a glance over his shoulder. The Count was still

running, arms going like pistons, chest heaving mightily with the effort. 'That's it, Count! Keep it—' Suddenly he ducked as a salvo of slugs cut the air just above his head. Now he waited no longer. With a deep breath, he sprang into the muddy water, gasping with the shock as its coolness struck him in the loins. The Count followed the next instant, disappearing beneath the surface and coming up stuttering, '*I can't swim, Otto!*'

'Well, now's your chance to learn!' Otto cried unfeelingly. 'Head for that clump of bushes over there on the left side. Come on – quick! I'll keep up with you to see you're all right.'

Together the two men headed across to the other side at an angle to the bridge, which was now filled with a mass of dead and dying men and animals, their cries of rage and pain mingling with the shrilling of many whistles and the clatter of heavy nailed boots. Otto didn't need to look up to know what the noise indicated: the bulls were arriving on the scene.

'Come on, Count, get those arms working!' he cried, holding his head above the muddy water.

'I'm trying my best, Otto,' the Count spluttered.

'*Try more*, because if we aren't over there soon, what's left of us will be feeding the fishes!'

Five minutes later, with the chatter of heavy machine-guns indicating that the military police were now at the bridge in full force, the two of them reached the other side and collapsed in the mud, gasping and spluttering like two aged asthmatics. They'd done it!

Half an hour later the skirmish was all over. The helmeted military policemen were now going stolidly from body to body, routinely placing their pistol muzzles at the base of the skulls of those who still groaned and blowing them to hell, meanwhile the officer behind the wheel of the big staff car pressed hard on his horn – evidently the Germans were hard on their heels. Then they were gone altogether, and a strange silence fell over the bridge, broken only by the strained, faint whimpers of the dying horses and the soft hush of the evening breeze; for now night was beginning to sweep down slowly along the water, casting eerie shadows on the mud banks.

Otto spoke at last, glad to hear the sound of his own voice; there was something uncanny about the sight of the bullet-pocked bridge surrounded by massacred artillerymen.

'Count, I suggest we go up there and find what we can in the way of dry clothes – and maybe if we're lucky, something to get our biters into. My old guts are doing back-flips with hunger!'

'Rob the dead, Otto?' the Count asked, aghast.

'Well, those poor stiffs won't be needing it any more, will they?' Otto said, with more courage than he felt. 'Come on, let's see if we can find ourselves a slab of that dried pork the Popovs are always eating.'

The Count refused – with unusual firmness for him. Instead, he stood guard in the growing darkness, brandishing Otto's pistol, while the latter, repressing his desire to vomit, flitted from corpse to corpse in search of food. Already he had given up his original plan to strip dry clothing off the bodies sprawled out on the bridge; his taut nerves wouldn't allow him to do *that*.

In the last of the light, the corpses looked horrible, their faces and hands already a dead, greenish colour with strange blotches of yellow on them, like beef hung up in the butcher's for a few days. And yet somehow, to Otto, the slaughtered artillerymen didn't seem dead. He had the feeling that they were watching him from their almost closed eyes; there was something hideous and uncanny in their grisly, shining gazes. In the end he gave up. He had found a mouldy loaf of black bread, an end of stale salami and a flask of cold tea mixed with vodka. That would have to do; he couldn't stand the sight of those faces any longer.

He rose to his feet, his booty clutched to his damp chest, trying not to look at the corpses, which seemed to leer up at him knowingly. 'Let's get out of here, Count,' he called softly, somehow unable to bring himself to raise his voice, as if it might rouse the dead to life again. 'Let's make dust. This place is putting years on me.'

The Count didn't react. He was staring at the bullet-pocked road-sign at the far end of the bridge, pistol fallen to his hip, as if he had just received a great shock.

'Count,' Otto hissed urgently, 'I'm talking to you. What's the matter? You got tin ears or something?'

The Count shook himself like a man trying to rouse himself from a deep sleep. 'Can you see what I see on that sign, Otto? The name I mean?'

'Of course I can't!' Otto snorted impatiently. 'You know the Popovs write everything arse-first. No wonder they make such a fuck-up of things.'

'Try, Otto, my eyes aren't as good as they were.'

'Great crap on the Christmas tree, are you going meschugge now—'

'Please, Otto.'

'All right, all right,' Otto said, 'anything to humour you, as long as we make dust out of this place quick. First there's an "M" and then there's one of those "H"s with a list to port.'

' "I".' The Count supplied the letter with growing excitement. 'Go on.'

'Then that "R" of theirs – reads as "P", don't it?'

'Yes . . . go on, Otto.'

' "O". Oh, *no* – MIROPOL!' Otto gasped.

'Yes, yes! And it's only two kilometres away from here!' the Count exclaimed delightedly. 'I tell you, my boy, it's—' he stuttered in his attempt to find the right word, '— *kismet!*'

THREE

They were crouching in the musty-smelling kitchen of one of the little fishermen's cottages which lined the bank of the canal, eating the cold sausage and black bread, and washing the stale fare down with drinks from the canteen of tea and vodka. They had broken in by the rear door, entering cautiously from the vegetable garden after standing watch over the place for fifteen minutes from the cover of the sunflowers, which in Russia always formed a hedge around the house. It had been empty, they had concluded. Obviously the owner had been smart enough to realize that a house near a bridge would be a prime target for the *Luftwaffe*'s bombers, and had fled while the going was good.

Now all was quiet outside, save for the silver rustle of the harnesses of the dead horses in the night wind and the sound of an abandoned dog howling at the yellow, glowing disc of the harvest moon. They ate in silence, each man preoccupied with his own thoughts. Occasionally Otto would glance at the Count; he guessed from his quick answering look that the older man was eager to talk about Miropol, but Otto had no intention of letting him do so. Instead, he kept his face blank of interest, indeed of all emotion. At that moment he felt strangely detached, possessed by a kind of melancholy, his soul seemingly banished from his body.

Was it the impact of the events of the last few days which had left him feeling so drained? Or was it Russia itself, this vast, crazy country, that induced his mood? He didn't know. But it was a mood he would often experience in

Russia in years to come – a feeling of being lost, insignificant, of complete unimportance in this limitless country.

The Count took the plunge at long last. 'Otto, you know we must try. That we must do at least!'

Otto knew well what his companion meant, but he was determined not to help him in any way; the Count would have to spell it out.

'The Miropol Position,' the Count said, a little awkwardly.

'What about it?' Otto asked tonelessly, keeping his eyes fixed on the flask in his hand.

'We *can't* just sit here and let them be massacred. Whatever you think of their allegiance to the Third Reich, Otto, they are young men – and they're Germans like us.'

Otto thought of the young men he had seen being trained back in that Godforsaken place in Rumania: blond fools with open innocent faces – men who were only too eager to die for 'Folk, Fatherland and Führer'. 'All right, Count,' he snapped petulantly, 'speak your piece and get it over with.'

The Count beamed at him. 'Let me tell you something about big guns, Otto. Now, they look like pretty impressive pieces of machinery, don't they?'

Otto said nothing.

'Made of high-quality steel, weighing tons – you would think there were nothing a puny human being could do against them unless he had gun cotton, high explosive and so on – which, as you rightly pointed out, we do *not* possess.' Again he paused, as if he half-expected Otto to say something.

But Otto remained obstinately silent.

'Yet, like all man-made things, they have their weakness. In this case the weakness is that the whole thing depends upon an object you could slip into your trouser pocket without it ever being noticed – the firing pin.'

'Firing pin?'

'Yes. Look.' Bending down, he traced a square object in the dust of the kitchen floor. 'That is roughly the shape of the breech-block, which fits into the breech of a big gun and carries out the job of firing the thing, once the shell and propellant have been inserted. Now here, in the middle of that breech-block –' again he bent and scratched an 'X' in the middle of the block '– is the firing pin, a small locking device with a steel pin in its centre. Without it, the most massive product of Krupps *cannot be fired*.' His eyes narrowed and he lowered his voice for effect. 'And a firing pin can be removed from a gun in seconds, simply by turning the locking device anti-clockwise.' He made a twisting gesture. 'Just like that, Otto.' He stopped and looked at the young man opposite him, as if fully expecting a burst of rapturous applause.

He didn't receive it. Instead, Otto sighed. 'So that's it, eh? We're to remove the firing pins at Miropol?'

'Exactly.'

'And what are the crews supposed to be doing, Count, while we stroll into their bunkers with a friendly "Good day and it's nice weather for the time of the year and we've just popped by to sabotage your guns. Won't be half a mo and then we'll be on our way again"?' Otto's face contorted cynically. 'Oh, come on, Count, do grow up! Where have you been for the last hundred years – in a shitting convent?'

The Count was not offended. 'Of course, I know it won't be easy. But the point I was trying to make is that two brave and bold men could attempt to knock those monsters out *without* high explosives and the like.'

'Where did you get that "two brave and bold men" bit?'

'My dear boy. I know that beneath that veneer of cynicism and cowardice you cultivate, there beats the heart of a lion.'

Otto groaned.

'Now, I'd like to ask you a question, Otto. What uniform are those poor chaps lying dead on the bridge wearing?'

'How the hell do I know? I'm just a stupid civilian.'

The Count answered his own question. 'Well, I shall tell you, Otto. They are artillerymen and they are wearing the uniform of the Red Army's artillery. Now that is the same uniform worn by the men manning the batteries at Miropol. Listen,' he continued urgently, as if he was really determined to convince Otto that his plan was feasible, 'you saw the terrible confusion on that bridge this afternoon. You know the kind of chaos that has been reigning in this country ever since the invasion. So who would question us if we appeared at the Miropol Position dressed in the same uniform as the soldiers there?'

'All right, I'll buy it, Count. We *might* get in without being discovered. But what then? Even the Popovs, demoralized and disorganized as they are, *must* have guards in those bunkers. They know the value of those defensive positions up there as well as we do.'

'Agreed, Otto, but what was it the Great Napoleon said? *L'audace – er, l'audace* . . .' the Count's face fell suddenly. 'Oh, I've forgotten the rest.'

'No matter – you're no Napoleon, and I don't know what the hell "*l'audace*" means in the first place. But we've got to have something more than just a hope, Count!'

The Count looked hard at him. 'I'll think of something, Otto, never fear. You know me.'

'Yes,' Otto replied sourly. 'That's just what's worrying me.'

The Count ignored the comment. 'But in essence you'll go along with me? Do I understand that from your comments?'

'All right, all right, Count, I'll sleep on it, let's say that. Now I'm going to hit the sack.'

Five minutes later Otto was fast asleep, while the Count stared thoughtfully at the flaking ceiling of the little kitchen . . .

It was three o'clock the following morning when the Count woke Otto out of a deep sleep with an excited cry. 'I've got it, Otto! I've got it!'

'Got what?'

'How to do it.' He shook Otto harder, as if he wasn't sure whether he was really awake. 'Of getting into those gun bunkers.'

Otto sat up with a groan, licking parched lips; the tea and vodka must have been stronger than he'd thought. 'Can't it wait, Count?' he moaned. 'It's the middle of the night, you know.'

'No, it can't, Otto. Time's running out. We've got to be up and about this business before dawn.'

Otto yawned. 'Give it to me then, and let's get the shitting nonsense over with.'

Hurriedly, the words tumbling furiously from his mouth, the Count explained the plan he had dreamed up while Otto had been snoring; then, with a self-satisfied smile, he stopped and awaited Otto's verdict.

Otto took his time. Outside the same crazed, abandoned dog howled at the moon, whose light now filtered a honey-yellow through the cracks in the shutters. Finally, when it seemed that the Count would soon explode if he didn't speak soon, Otto took a deep breath. 'Well, I'll give you one thing, Count. You seem to have assessed the Russian character right. They do like their sauce better than anything – even better than female gash. But let me ask you this.'

'Yes, go on, Otto – ask away, my dear boy.'

'Where are you going to find the marie to buy this sauce with, eh? Tell me that.'

The Count grinned. Like a conjuror, he suddenly produced two gleaming gold roubles from between his fingers. 'With these, my boy.'

Otto could hardly contain his surprise. 'How come you've still got those? The Cossacks must have pinched mine when I was unconscious, before they took me to Olga's hospital.'

'In the Abwehr, we learned how to conceal such precious

things about our person in a way that would not be noticeable during a casual search.'

'You mean, *up there*?'

'I do indeed.'

'Then you must be the ass that shat the golden ducats.'[1] Otto burst out laughing.

The Count joined in. 'Of course, dear Otto. Now, are you with me?' He held out his hand.

Otto took it and said, still grinning, 'Count, I know I want my head examining, but what can you do with an ass like you? Especially when he shits vodka . . .'

[1] There is an old German fairy-story of a donkey which excretes golden coins.

FOUR

On the 27th June 1941, several disparate things happened in Western Russia which, although considered unlinked and relatively unimportant at the time, contributed significantly to the defeat of Hitler's vaunted 'one thousand year Reich'. In years to come, Herr Otto Stahl would often say, after his morning *piccolo* of champagne – in his old age he is afflicted with blood pressure, though he snorts that 'it's only pins and needles' and drinks the champagne for that reason – 'June 27th marks the day that Adolf lost the war.'

Few would be so dogmatic about it as Otto – but then, as an old man he has become dogmatic about most things. Yet, when one looks at the events of that day, one can see how together they *did* stop the Bodyguard's advance. Had the Germans succeeded in capturing the Caucasus, and its oil, there is little doubt that it would have meant the defeat of Soviet Russia.

The burningly hot day started off with an unfortunate accident to General von Manstein, the Army Commander. Realizing that he was now operating far in advance of his main headquarters and might run into partisans, the good General decided he would arm himself with a pistol. Unhappily, he had long forgotten how carefully pistols should be handled. Thus, while buckling it on with morning-stiff and clumsy fingers he managed to shoot himself in the left buttock. As Hitler commented later when he heard of the accident: 'All Southern Russia wide open for the taking, and what does my Commander-in-Chief there do? Shoots himself in the arse! Doubtless in an attempt to blow his brains out.' The Führer allowed the polite titter of laughter from his staff to die away, then added, 'He can't have missed by much!' Again his staff had laughed. The Führer's bullet-headed toady and secretary Martin Bormann immediately noted the remark, for inclusion in the book of the Führer's witticisms and *bon mots* he planned to compile after the victorious conclusion of the war. It would be entitled: *Fun with the Führer:* the *Humour of Adolf Hitler*, and would undoubtedly be a world bestseller. It would also make him a great deal of money – and Bormann liked money.

This unfortunate accident meant that von Manstein would spend the next forty-eight-hour tour of his vast command lying on his stomach in the back of a halftrack – something which didn't improve his always rather volatile temper. Thus it was that when a handsome young officer courier from General Dietrich appeared to ask how to approach the next major obstacle in his path, von Manstein barked, 'What obstacle, Lieutenant? Well, don't stand there like a dummy. Haven't you ever seen a wounded general before?'

'Yes . . . er, no, sir,' the officer stuttered, staring down at the General, who was lying face-down on a blanket in the back of the halftrack, with his crimson-striped pants down about his ankles and a large piece of sticking plaster attached to his skinny pale rump. 'The Miropol Position – that's our next objective. My General says he knows almost nothing about it.'

Von Manstein sneered. 'Ah, *your* General feels he is a little in the dark about the situation to his front, does he?'

'Yessir,' the lieutenant said bravely.

'Well tell him from me that his Army Commander, Erich von Manstein, is *completely* in the dark – completely, totally! The maps are all wrong. Nothing is right. I know as much about what lies in front of me as the simplest, chuckle-headed stubble-hopper out there, getting his turnip blown off by the Popovs! *Ordannanz,*' he bellowed angrily, 'take a message for General Dietrich!'

One hour later, Dietrich was reading von Manstein's message, his broad face darkening by the instant as his dark-brown eyes scanned the irate Army Commander's message. Finally his rage broke forth. 'The Jewish whoreson, the shit-heel, that snobby-nosed arse with ears . . .'[1]

For a full five minutes Dietrich gave vent to an angry torrent of curses directed at his senior officer, until finally his officers dared to ask, 'What is it, sir?'

Dietrich took a deep breath; the hand with which he held the message was trembling violently. 'I'll tell you,' he gasped finally. 'Listen to this.' Controlling himself with difficulty, he read out the contents of the message. ' "If the Führer's beloved Bodyguard feels its skin is too precious to advance without one hundred per cent intelligence about the enemy's positions, which are probably held by a bunch of ruptured Russian militia, then I suggest the Bodyguard dig in and have a good rest, while the poor flat-footed stubble-hoppers of the *Wehrmacht* do the job of taking Miropol for them . . ." ' He broke off, unable to contain his anger. 'By all that is holy, gentlemen,' he cried, his crimson face staring up at his tall young officers, 'that message is little better than high treason! "If the Führer's beloved Bodyguard feels its skin is too precious . . . ruptured Russian militia . . ." ' he repeated, beating his brow dramatically. It was perhaps beneficial for General Dietrich's health that just at that moment a diversion occurred. Captain Peiper appeared with a group of armoured cars from his reconnaissance battalion, followed by several hundred dirty, bearded Russian riders; leading them was an officer whose face was covered by red marks, as if he had been lashed by a whip, and who wore the green cross badge of the NKVD.

'Deserters, Standartenführer,' Peiper reported, spring-

[1] Von Manstein, whose original name had been V. Lewinski was suspected in some quarters of being a Jew.

ing easily from the side of his armoured car, arrogantly
oblivious, or so it seemed, to Dietrich's obvious rage and
the worried looks on the faces of his senior officers. 'Claim
to be Don Cossacks. Want to join us as allies in order to
free their homeland.'

'My God, Peiper,' Dietrich cried, 'you've been in the SS
long enough to know how to report correctly—' Suddenly
he broke off, his curiosity getting the better of his anger;
it wasn't every day that an officer of the NKVD surren-
dered. It was well known now among the Red Army that
Hitler had ordered all captured political commissars and
NKVD officers to be shot immediately. 'Bring the officer
over. I want to talk to him.'

Thus it was that Dietrich discovered for the first time
what had happened to his two agents, Count von der Weide
and Otto Stahl – for the NKVD officer was, naturally,
none other than Petrov. In due course he was dismissed to
the Division's prisoner-of-war cage. Much later he would
be released to join Russian General Vlassov's renegade
anti-Soviet army and would be duly hanged in Moscow as
a traitor in 1945.

Now Dietrich called an immediate conference of his
senior regimental and battalion commanders and told them
his thoughts on the Miropol Position.

'It appears, gentlemen, that our two Abwehr men must
have discovered something. They escaped after being taken
prisoner, but being the stout fellows they are, they have
not attempted to flee to the nearest German unit. No –
they are still obviously working at their mission.' Dietrich
narrowed his eyes against the sun, which was already
blazing down. 'Why?' Dietrich answered his own question
almost immediately. 'Because they have discovered that
there is something – something very unpleasant – waiting
for us at Miropol.' He paused for effect and allowed his
words to sink in. 'What that is, I do not know. Therefore
I am not going to allow myself to be goaded into ill-
considered action by that swine von Manstein. The Divi-

sion halts until I hear from the agents or obtain definite information about the situation there. Unfortunately, we are a new formation; we cannot allow those old farts of the Wehrmacht to sneer at us for being too cautious. Therefore, we must also make an attempt to find out what is up there ourselves.' He looked around at the circle of serious young faces. 'Gentlemen, I am asking for a volunteer to take out a long-range patrol.'

Major Kurt Meyer, hard-faced, fanatical-eyed, instantly opened his mouth, but his second-in-command Gerd Bremer beat him to it. 'I'll go, sir!' he bellowed, shouting as he always did as if he were back on the parade ground in Berlin-Lichterfelde.

Dietrich made a show of clasping his hands over his ears, while Meyer glowered at his big young subordinate; Bremer now affected a thin moustache, presumably in imitation of Dietrich's. 'All right, Bremer, you've got the mission. But none of your little Hussar tricks this time, please.'

'I promise, Standartenfuhrer,' Bremer roared, flushing with pleasure. 'What are my orders?'

'Very simple. Push with your motor-cycle company as close as you can to Miropol and report back with your findings. Now,' he warned, 'remember this, Bremer. It's a look-see, run-and-report mission. Don't attempt to cure your throat-ache on this mission.' He touched the Knight's Cross dangling at his throat, to indicate fully what he meant.

The others laughed. They all knew the ambitious twenty-two-year-old Captain was desperately eager to win the same decoration himself before the campaign ended.

Bremer smiled back good-humouredly. 'Don't worry, sir. I'll carry out your orders to the letter.'

But the Bremers of this world never listen to orders. Thus it was that some time later, another fateful event was added to the strange pattern of happenings that June day. Racing flat out with his company of motor-cyclists, a machine-gunner leaning out of each side-car, Bremer led his men straight into a trap some five kilometres to the front of the Bodyguard's position. The details of that little skirmish and the long-drawn out firefight which followed are relatively unimportant, except possibly for those elderly German ladies still drawing a generous war widow's pension from the Bonn government for the death of husbands in that nameless spot. One detail, however, has to be recorded – one of Bremer's men was captured.

It was part of the Bodyguard's creed never to allow a wounded man to fall into the hands of the enemy, especially the Russians; indeed, later in the war, officers would shoot their seriously wounded subordinates rather than allow them to fall into Soviet hands. Twice on the day in question, Bremer personally led desperate charges to break into the Soviet position where Rottenführer Heidweiler was held prisoner; twice he was driven back with further losses. Finally he gave in. Some time later, the Russians allowed the seriously wounded corporal to be transported to the rear for attention; at this stage of the war it was not yet their practice to slaughter SS prisoners immediately on capture.

Rottenführer Heidweiler, his left arm shot away, a great gaping hole in his right leg where a burst of Russian machine-gun fire had caught him, didn't know this. He was still in a complete state of shock, crazy with fear, and tense with explosive emotion. On the way to Romanov's Eighth General Hospital, he broke the glass window of the horse-drawn ambulance and tried to slash the unsuspecting driver's throat. The Russian wounded had immediately set upon him, and he had gone completely berserk until one of them had finally clubbed him with the stick he was using as a crutch. He had arrived at the Hospital unconscious.

Some time later he had awakened. Olga had done what she could for him, but now, what with the huge numbers of wounded who were passing through her hands, drugs and medical supplies were beginning to give out. All around Heidweiler saw rows and rows of Russians lying on the floor, groaning, moaning, calling out for their '*matka*', urinating in the straw on which they lay. The air was heavy with the hospital smell of spiritous disinfectant.

Again the Rottenführer had panicked. The moans, the cries, the pleas, the strange guttural curses – all reminded him that he was in the hands of the Bolsheviks. He knew all too well what they did to prisoners, especially if they belonged to the Waffen SS? Hadn't he seen with his own eyes the corpses of the two NCOs from his own division who had been captured on the first day of the great offensive and whose sexual organs had been sliced off and placed in their mouths? Instinctively he felt for his own penis. It was still there. But for how long? *No! He wouldn't let them!* He lurched from the straw mattress onto the urine-wet floor. No one took the least notice of him. He started to crawl. A big, burly woman in a blood-stained nurse's uniform who was attending to a groaning boy's wounds – one eye was a purple, suppurating pit – flung him a look, then shrugged and went back to her task, hitting the boy with her free hand every time he jogged her.

In a kind of pain-racked dream, Rottenführer Heidweiler started to follow his nose, trying to find his way by smell to the hospital's lab. Once, before the war, he had worked briefly in a Berlin hospital; he knew the lab would contain what he needed for his purpose, which was to set the hospital ablaze before they began those fearful experiments with their razor-sharp scalpels on his defenceless loins. Better dead than half a man. He crawled on.

A corridor with the recent dead piled high on both sides, ready to be disposed of in the open lime pits behind the hospital. Orderlies in blood-stained rubber aprons and boots, but naked underneath in the heat, hurrying back and forth from the operating theatres, casually bearing baskets full of sawn-off, amputated limbs . . . In his crazed fantasy, Heidweiler thought they were severed human sexual organs. He crawled on faster. No one took the least notice of him. Men were always crawling about the Eighth; there simply weren't enough nurses and orderlies to go round.

A door swung open. Suddenly Heidweiler's nostrils were assailed by a strong smell of chemicals. *The lab!* The door closed again, but he had it now. He crawled on desperately. Ignoring the burning pain in his wrecked arm, he pushed open the door. A line of phials containing human shit met his eyes: dysentery samples – he knew them well. No use for him. Then he had what he sought. Bottle after bottle of ether! His strength fading rapidly now, he crawled over to them, leaving a sticky trail of black blood on the floor behind him. He pulled down the first bottle. It crashed to the floor and smashed. Instantly floods of ether gas assailed his nostrils. It didn't matter. He pulled down another and another, and then, just as his head began to turn and turn and turn, he pulled down the bunsen burner from the lab table so that it dropped into the flood of ether. His last impression before he dropped unconscious was that the world was coming to an end . . .

Desperately, Olga, her hands burnt, her face black with smoke, her eyebrows and hair singed, pulled the wounded man free. He was one of the blinded ones, his face a black crusted mask streaked with caked blood, and two vivid, scarlet pools instead of eyes. Dragging him on to the grass outside the hospital and ripping off her skirt, she beat out the greedy little blue flames that leapt up along the length of his charred uniform.

But he was only one. In the grounds of the blazing hospital there were hundreds of them, hopping along on their stumps or being dragged behind their comrades, fighting off the flames which followed. All of them were screaming piteously.

Fifty metres away, the wounded men had formed a

pyramid and were desperately trying to clamber up on the shoulders of their fellows and scale the high wall that cut them off from safety. Supporting themselves with crutches, spades, sticks, they hobbled towards it, trying to fight their way across, their rags already blazing a raspberry-red, roaring, screaming, cursing and finally giving off one last frenzied, desperate shriek as the flames consumed them.

The local fire engine from Romanov stood powerless nearby. Its engine was still running, but the firemen were all dead, suffocated almost immediately they had reached the scene. Now their uniforms were crumbling in the baking heat, leaving them naked and rigid in their seats, perched against the metal ladder, their bodies blackened and their helmets glowing red on their heads.

When the horror was over and the last of the terribly burnt men had sunk into blessed oblivion at last, Olga sat down and cried – cried as she had not done since the day the drunken White had raped her, all those years ago, her hefty shoulders heaving pathetically while her weary nurses, their faces as black as hers, stared at her hopelessly.

In the end she pulled herself together. Slowly, she wiped away the tears that ran down that plain, homely pudding-face of hers and rose to her feet. The others waited while across the way what was left of their hospital continued to burn a gorgeous lemon-yellow. Olga took her time, forcing her exhausted brain to think things out. That Fritz had done it, of course, the one with 'Adolf Hitler' scrawled on the black armband of death on his sleeve – the same Adolf Hitler to whom her betrayer Otto had sworn allegiance, too. They were all the same, the Fritzes. They took the most precious thing a weak woman could offer a man and then walked away, laughing cynically. Not only that, they were ruthless killers – arsonists who murdered helpless, wounded men and women.

Suddenly there was a look of new determination on her face; somehow it seemed at that moment hollowed out by the leaping flames, no longer so pudding-like, but grim, firm and determined. Deliberately she pulled off her blackened, torn doctor's overall and dropped it to the body-littered ground while the others stared at her in wonder.

'Comrades,' she said, her voice quiet but very firm. 'The time has come to fight the fascists. We have done all we can to tend the sick and wounded.' She shrugged. 'Our hospital is no more – we have no supplies, nor is there any hope of getting any.'

'But what shall we do?' asked a burly nurse. It was the same one who, in a different age, had grabbed Otto's eggs as he had bent over the sink.

'We shall fight them, we weak women who have been abused by them; in particular we shall fight those blond beasts who bear the hated name of their thrice-accursed Führer on their arms – the Bodyguard. They will be our special enemies from now onwards. We shall hunt them down and kill them like mad dogs.' She spat on the ground in disgust. Pulling out her little duty pistol, she flourished it over her head in sudden light-headed enthusiasm. 'Death to the invader! Death to the fascist! *Death to the murderers of the Adolf Hitler Bodyguard!*'

Fired by their Colonel's enthusiasm, the women echoed her cries fiercely.

The few men who had survived the holocaust, and who lay slumped apathetically on the charred turf, stared in wonder at these new Amazons – but the women had no time for the men. All was frantic haste as they followed Olga's order to find military clothing and weapons. Ripping their female gear from their hefty bodies, they revealed massive flanks clad in red flannel, and breasts that trembled beneath their vests like big jellies. As they struggled into what male clothing they could tug from the dead, rolling the corpses over unfeelingly as they searched them for weapons, they seemed to be carried away by some over-whelming excitement, known only to themselves.

Finally they were ready and formed up in rough order,

awaiting Olga's command. To other eyes they might have appeared ludicrous in their bulky ill-fitting uniforms, their rifles held at an awkward slope on their shoulder – a caricature of real soldiers, maybe. But the handful of watching men didn't laugh. There was something fanatical about the fervent look of the women as they stared at Olga. And it would have ill behoved the men to laugh, for that evening they were witnessing the birth of Russia's most feared partisan unit, one which would win everlasting glory in the history of the Great Patriotic War: Red Olga's Partisan Guards.

'Forward, comrades!' Olga commanded at last.

'Death to the Fascists!' one of them cried.

'Death to the Fascists!' The cry was taken up by a hundred and one female throats. Then they were stumbling out of the hospital grounds and into the growing darkness, most of them awkward and out of step, marching into history . . .

June 27th 1941 was over at last. The long chain of events of that day had been completed. Unknown to anyone, save perhaps God – if he still had any time for the crazy war-torn world below – the fate of Nazi Germany had been sealed.

FIVE

Dawn!

Already it was scorching hot, and a blue heat-haze was rippling over the dusty steppe. The glare of the rising sun cut into the eyes of the two friends like a sharp blade.

Sweating and cursing with the effort, pausing every now and again to scratch irritably at his uniform – for the heat was making his friends the lice particularly active – Otto heaved at the handcart, which was laden with bottles of pepper vodka bought from a Jew in the last village. The Count, meanwhile, dressed in the uniform of a sergeant in the Soviet artillery, strode out in front of him, unburdened by anything but the round-barrelled tommy-gun he carried jauntily over his shoulder. As he had explained back at the canal, 'The Russians are very hot on the privileges of rank, you see, Otto. They'd tumble to us at once if they saw me helping you with the cart.'

'Little blokes always get their nose rubbed in it!' Otto had said sourly. 'One law for the rich again, I suppose. But I thought this was the classless society? You know, everybody equal and all that sort of thing.'

'Ah, indeed. But that is just the theory, my boy,' he beamed at Otto. 'You know the old saying; the biggest animals pick the sweetest fruit. I doubt if it is any different in the Soviet workers' paradise.'

'Well, why are you the shitting sergeant and me the humble toiler?' Otto had attempted one last protest.

'I suppose because I was born to command—'

'Ballocks!'

So it was that Otto now toiled up the trail behind the

Count dragging the handcart. They were now getting ever closer to the height on which were mounted the fearsome cannon, but approaching them from a different angle from the first time. Once more the huge guns came into view; again they paused and gawped in awed silence at the long, menacing barrels, wondering if it would really be possible for two puny human beings like themselves to deal with them. Again, too, they noted the lack of activity round about; it was as if the Miropol Position was empty of soldiers. For a while Otto tried to fool himself that it, too, might have been abandoned by the panic-stricken, fleeing Red Army, like so many other fortified positions over the last few days. Five minutes later he found out to his dismay that it wasn't so.

As they turned a bend in the trail, they saw that infantry were dug in everywhere below the guns and to their immediate front. Otto paused and said gloomily, 'There are plenty of them, Count.'

The Count's gaze swept the steep slope, taking in the machine-gun posts covering the openings in the concertina wire – obviously they were positioned so as to lead any attacking infantry right up to their fixed fields of fire. Further back were sand-bagged positions containing mortar crews, guarded by little bunches of infantrymen, dug-in and smoking in a bored manner as they enjoyed the morning sun. 'A mini-Verdun,' he commented finally. 'But as the Prussians used to say, "many enemies, much honour".'

'Something I could do without, thank you very much.'

'One thing though, Otto,' the Count said as they resumed their progress up the slope. 'By the look of them they're Tartars or Siberians, something like that – men who get drunk easily and speak the tongue of Tolstoy as badly as I do.'

'Let's hope you're right, Count, because your whole plan stinks. I've heard those slant-eyed gents have some

nasty habits with their knives when they get prisoners in
their paws. I'd hate to end up as a singing tenor.'

The Count shuddered dramatically. 'Don't even think
of things like that, Otto, I beg you!'

Now they started to ascend a well-trodden path, which
wound its way around to the back of the massive bunkers.
Otto guessed it was used to bring up supplies in case the
main road was held by the enemy.

'Even the best infantry would have difficulty getting up
here,' the Count panted, his handsome face flushed with
the exertion of the climb; little pearls of sweat glistened in
his bushy eyebrows. 'It would be Fort Douamont[1] all over
again.'

Otto didn't reply. He couldn't; the path was so steep
that he needed all his energies to tow the cart; when the
cart's wooden wheels hit a rock and an electric shock ran
along his blistered palms – which happened frequently –
he didn't even have the strength to curse.

Now they could see the rear of the gun-bunkers quite
clearly; a low tunnel led into the concrete turret itself,
curving up at an angle so as to stop the blast of a detonation
rushing straight inside and to thwart any flame-thrower
crew who managed to live long enough to sneak up on the
place from behind.

'So much for Hairless Horst,' Otto told himself, fervently wishing he was back in that cosy, sleepy little
garrison town in Rumania, practising the 'two-backed
beast' with Gerda, instead of risking his neck in this crazy
plan of the Count's. For a moment, he considered asking
the other man if they couldn't simply turn back and make
a run for it while there was still time. But already time had
run out for them.

Suddenly a slant-eyed, pock-marked yellow face popped
up from a boulder to the right, and the old Russian
challenge '*Stoi?*' broke the heavy morning stillness. A long-

[1] One of the Verdun forts which claimed thousands of German lives
but was eventually taken in 1916.

bayoneted rifle pointed in their direction, but Otto was pleased to see that the young Siberian, or whatever he was, was merely acting routinely.

The Count beamed at the young soldier in the manner of a benevolent uncle. 'Vodka,' he said, taking one of the half-litre bottles of pepper vodka from the cart which Otto was towing and tendering it to the sentry like a policeman trying to tempt a trapped cat down from a tree.

The sentry's coal-black eyes glittered and he licked his lips. 'Me?' he asked, pointing a thumb at his chest.

The Count nodded eagerly like a lunatic. 'You!'

Eagerly the sentry grabbed it. Resting the bayonet between his knees, he tapped the neck of the bottle against the nearest rock, snapped it off, raised it to his lips, took a tentative sip, spat out a few glass splinters from his lips, and then took a long, deep pull of the fiery spirits. With a casual gesture and a broad wink, he waved them on, and they walked by, leaving him gargling happily with the vodka.

The Count smiled at Otto and winked. 'Didn't I tell you, Otto, my boy? Our friends the Russians would sell their mothers for vodka.'

'Let's hope you're right,' Otto gasped. They were almost at the bunker now.

'Now, Otto,' the Count said, speaking out of the side of his mouth, 'you've done enough. Just keep that gang up there happy with the fire-water and I'll do the rest.' He jerked a thumb at the group of gunners sitting outside their bunker, some naked to the waist, watching them approach with obvious interest.

'What do you mean, you'll do the rest, you silly old fart?' Otto asked urgently, for he liked the Count and the last thing he wanted was to see him harmed.

'You know nothing about big guns – you wouldn't even be able to find the firing pins. I'll sneak inside and do the dirty work – all right?'

Otto shook his head in mock disgust, but there was nothing he could do about it.

'All right, Otto, now you're on your own,' the Count hissed, as a slant-eyed Siberian started to rise to meet them, his black, unwinking Oriental eyes fixed on the bottles in the cart.

The Count acknowledged their interest in grand style, striding purposefully towards the group, crying, 'Vodka, little brothers! Vodka from Comrade Stalin!'

Otto hurried after him anxiously. The Count seemed to be really enjoying himself in his role of bringer of gifts from the Soviet dictator; the silly shit simply hadn't any idea of the danger they were in. Before he had a chance to restrain his companion Otto found himself busily handing out bottles to the greedy little yellow men, who hurried off with their precious burdens clasped to their skinny chests, as if desperately afraid that some comrade might snatch it from them before they could taste the contents.

Within minutes the Siberians were keening drunkenly to themselves, their black eyes already blank and glazed-looking, rocking from side to side in discreet Oriental ecstasy and taking routine measured gulps at their bottles. Watching them, Otto felt fear tinged with awe: how *could* men get drunk that quickly?

'Done it!' the Count gasped, back at his side once again, his face flushed with triumph.

'Where is it?'

'What?'

'The shitting firing pin!' Otto exclaimed.

The Count winked. 'Slight change of plan. Instead of taking it and leaving a hole in the breech-block which they'd spot straight away and perhaps replace, I simply took the pin out and smashed it against the side of the cannon. Then I put it back again. Not bad, eh?'

Otto didn't reply. The Count might be a genius, but Otto knew him of old; it wasn't wise to flatter his vanity.

'Not bad, eh?' the Count repeated hopefully.

'All right,' Otto conceded grudgingly, 'as that old whore my mother, the Witch, would say – you ain't from yesterday, Count.'

The Count beamed down at his nails with mock modesty. 'High praise indeed, Otto – thank you.'

'Come on,' Otto urged, feeling for the first time that the Count's crazy scheme might succeed after all, and they passed on, leaving the Siberians behind them getting steadily drunker in stoic silence.

The next bunker proved equally easy. Vodka, it seemed, was the key to all doors in Soviet Russia. The Siberian gunners rose to the free alcohol like trout to a succulent fly. They asked no questions; simply accepted their bottles, walked away and settled down to the serious task of getting as drunk as possible.

'Shit on the shingle!' Otto hissed to the Count in wonder, 'I've seen some sauce-hounds in my time – Berlin-Wedding was full of them – but nothing like this. No questions, no nothing – just straight to the sauce, as if it was mother's milk.' He shook his head in wonder.

'It must be something to do with the immensity of Russia, I shouldn't wonder,' the Count said obscurely. 'But let us be grateful for the fact.' They passed on.

Five minutes later the Count emerged from the third bunker, face flushed with success again, and winked. 'Two to go now, Otto,' he breathed urgently. 'Soon be over with it. Luck's on our side, my boy.'

But it was not to be. Now their luck had finally run out.

Just as they halted outside the fourth bunker and the Count began to launch into his patter, a squat, barrel-chested Siberian with the heavy square epaulettes of an officer appeared, apparently from nowhere, and stared at them, hands on hips, obviously disgusted.

'Look at Ghenghis Khan over there,' Otto whispered hurriedly out of the corner of his mouth. 'The way he's looking at us gets the old piss trickling down the side of my leg.'

'Yes, he does look a bit like what one would imagine Ghenghis Khan might look like with that whispy –'

'– Knock it off, you silly old shit,' Otto interrupted him hastily, his heart beating rapidly now with fear. 'Keep walking. Get on with your spiel. Give 'em the joy-juice – *quick!*'

The Count's confident look vanished. Hastily he handed over the first bottle of free vodka to an eager Siberian, while the officer looked on. Turning round nervously, Otto saw suspicion written all over his face.

Hurriedly the Siberian soldier marched off to find a private spot in which to drink it in peace. But he didn't get far. Just as he passed, the officer raised his hand, fingers outstretched and tightly clasped together. Like a cleaver the huge hand descended. The Siberian yelped with pain and dropped the bottle which shattered at his feet on a rock. The officer cried something at him in a language that even Otto knew wasn't Russian and slapped the crestfallen soldier across both cheeks in a casual manner; then he turned, leaving him standing there like a chastened school-boy and began to stride purposefully towards Otto and the Count.

Otto froze. 'Watch it, Count!' he hissed.

The barrel-chested officer stopped a second soldier, also clutching his precious bottle. Again his hand chopped down. The bottle fell to the ground and shattered. '*Kak shal,*'[2] he grunted, a malicious grin in his eyes; plainly he wasn't sorry in the least.

The Count swallowed hard. The officer's hand had descended to the big pistol at his right hip. 'Otto, I think we've been rumbled.'

'You ain't wrong,' Otto hissed, and fumbled for the pistol he had concealed in the pocket of his baggy Red Army breeches.

Now the huge officer was standing in front of them, chest thrust out importantly, firing questions at them

[2] 'What a pity' in Russian.

which the red-faced Count, with his poor Russian, found quite impossible to answer.

The look of suspicion deepened in Genghis Khan's face. Otto knew now that it could only be a matter of seconds. He felt the hand holding the butt of the pistol go wet with sweat. He hated what he was going to have to do, but he knew there was no other way. Once again, it was kill or be killed.

Suddenly the officer stopped in the midst of a flood of questions. He turned his head and cried in Russian '*schpion*.'[3] Otto didn't need to understand Russian to know what he had said. In a single swift movement, he whipped out his pistol, clicked off the safety catch, and fired.

At that range he couldn't miss. The officer's head exploded, spattering the Siberians grouped all around with bright red blood and pieces of gleaming white skull. He fell immediately, his features slipping down his dying face like molten wax. The crowd of soldiers gave a great awed gasp. Desperately Otto looked around for some place to flee, while at his side the Count seemed transfixed, unable to move. One of the Siberians recovered from his shock. He wiped the blood from his yellow face and grabbed for his bayonet, his black eyes animated by rage and sudden hatred.

Otto didn't give him a chance to use it. His pistol barked again and the man reeled back, scarlet blood jetting from a wound in his shoulder. 'The gun bunker, Count!' Otto gasped. 'Make for it! Use yer tommy-gun . . . *Come on!*'

Together, their anxious gazes darting from side to side, Otto and the Count backed off towards the dark entrance to the gun-bunker, with the Siberians pressing forward menacingly after them. Otto raised his pistol threateningly every time he thought one or other of them might make a rush and try to outflank them.

Now they were almost there. Otto could sense their

[3] The German and Russian words for spy – *Spion* and *schpion* respectively – are virtually the same in their pronunciation.

position by the smell of the place – a combination of garlic, high-explosive powder, damp, and stale human sweat. Without taking his eyes off the Siberians for one moment, he nudged his companion: 'Count, you have a look-see at the entrance – see that there's no slimy shit waiting for us in the tunnel . . . Check how we can lock the doors behind us once we're in . . .'

'You'll be all right?'

'I'll be all right. *Now quick!* I've got four slugs left and that's enough if they decide to make a concerted rush.'

'I'm on my way, Otto.'

Reluctantly Otto slowed down somewhat, forcing himself not to turn tail and flee for his life. The Siberians pushed closer. He jerked his pistol from left to right, crouched low, legs spread apart, ready to fire at the first sign of a rush. He knew that once they summoned up courage and rushed him, he was finished. They'd swamp him.

Suddenly a grenade sailed through the air. With a start of fear Otto saw it roll to a stop close to his feet. Almost automatically, he kicked out at it, sending it sailing through the air, to land just in front of the Siberians. Next instant it exploded. Otto ducked. He could feel the hot air burning into the back of his skull. For one terrifying moment he thought his eardrums would burst with the noise. Blood trickled from his nostrils. He shook his head, dizzy from the blast. To his front, half a dozen of the Siberians were lying on the churned-up ground, writhing and moaning with pain.

'Count!' he called urgently. 'Are we there?'

'We're there!' the Count called back.

'Fine. Give the entrance a burst, then let's get out of here!'

'Do you think—'

'– Ape-turd!' Otto cried, his voice broken with fear. 'Do as I say! I can't hold this lot much longer.'

There was a flurry of 9mm slugs as the Count fired a

burst, then Otto was running backwards. He bumped into the Count. Together they staggered into the entrance of the bunker, which stank of explosive. From behind there came a roar of rage.

Swiftly Otto snapped off a couple of shots to left and right. A Siberian screamed and skidded to a sudden stop. But Otto had no eyes for him. 'Cover me, Count,' he gasped. 'I'll go—'

He broke off abruptly. To his right there was a dry, harsh chuckle. It saved his life. Hearing the sound, he whirled round, throwing his arm up to counter the expected thrust. A Siberian bayonet slit the length of his sleeve, drawing blood painfully. Reeling back, he gasped with the shock of it.

The Siberian, who had been hiding in the darkness of the entrance, chuckled again and plunged forward once more with his bayonet. Otto reacted instinctively. His right foot lashed out. The Siberian yelped in agony and fell forward, his hand still tightly clutching the bayonet. Otto grabbed for his skinny yellow arm. For what seemed an eternity, the two of them swayed back and forth, then with all his remaining strength, Otto brought the Siberian's hand down hard.

The Siberian screamed as his skinny wrist snapped like a dry twig cracking underfoot. Eyes blazing with fury he wrenched himself free. Otto followed through. Using his elbow as a bludgeon, he smashed it into his attacker's yellow face. He reeled against the wall, giving out muted growling noises. Carried away by rage, Otto hit him again. He gave one last shrill scream and then started to slide down the wall, eyes glazed. He was unconscious before he hit the floor.

'Come on, Otto!' the Count cried and grabbed his young friend, who was swaying to and fro as if he, too, might fall. 'Quick! We haven't much time left.'

Appalled by his own fury and shaken by the surprise attack, Otto allowed himself to be led down the dark corridor which led into the gun turret. In a daze he listened while the Count turned the screws which fastened the steel door behind them. Like a child he accepted a drink from a flask of cold tea and vodka, gulping the liquid down gratefully, while the older man supported his head like an anxious mother. Then, finally, he shook his head and began to become aware of his surroundings.

Squinting in the dim light he gazed at the great, gleaming breech of the cannon and the tall yellow shells stacked neatly to both sides of it. Then he said hopelessly, 'Count, now we're really up shit-street without a shovel.'

As the first burst of tommy-gun fire splattered against the steel door behind them, the Count nodded his head miserably in agreement. With unaccustomed vulgarity, he said tonelessly, 'Shit-street, indeed, my young friend . . .'

SIX

General Dietrich frowned.

He was staring once again at the aerial photographs that von Manstein had sent him that morning. They were of the Miropol Position – but all they revealed was that a trench-line had been dug recently on the western slope of the height. Nothing else. He turned to Lehmann, his chief of staff. 'You realize why that aristocratic shit sent us those Luftwaffe pictures, don't you?'

Lehmann nodded, but said nothing. As always, he was discreet. He knew perfectly well what von Manstein's intention had been. He had wanted to shame the Bodyguard into action. Undoubtedly he would soon be passing the word to the Führer's HQ that the Bodyguard was sitting on its thumbs, afraid to move on the Miropol Position.

Dietrich seemed to read his chief of staff's mind. 'I'd give him twenty-four hours, Lehmann. If we haven't moved by then, his pals up at Führer HQ will have been informed, and that wooden-arsed Keitel[1] will be only too eager to let the Führer know just how lily-livered his Bodyguard are. All of those Wehrmacht arse-holes up there hate our guts with a passion.' He shook his head. 'The Führer won't like it one bit.'

Lehmann spoke for the first time since they had studied the aerial photographs together. 'Standartenführer, I agree with you. The pictures are intended to put us on the spot, as you say. Either we move or the Führer discovers his Bodyguard is sitting on its bottom, while the Wehrmacht

[1] Hitler's chief military adviser.

bears the brunt of the fighting.' He nodded, as if he were confirming his own reasoning – a habit of his. 'Conclusion, Standartenführer—'

Dietrich beat him to it: 'Conclusion – the Bodyguard has to move, yes?'

'Yes.'

Again Dietrich frowned and tugged at the edge of his toothbrush moustache. 'I don't like it – I don't like it one bit, Lehmann. I have the same feeling I had in '18 at Château-Thierry. Our officers insisted the Amis wouldn't come – said they weren't prepared for action, that they were slow, needed a ton of chewing-gum per man before they attacked . . .' He chuckled drily at the memory of that battle, so long ago. 'But I knew they were wrong. I could smell trouble in the air.' He sniffed. 'And I can smell it now. I have a nasty feeling there's something very unpleasant waiting for us at Miropol.'

Lehmann listened attentively, as always. 'But, sir,' he said, when he knew his chief wanted him to speak, 'you know we can't just wait here. The war won't stop because – er – you and I have a premonition that something is wrong.' He looked straight at Dietrich. 'Quite frankly, sir, unless you do something soon the Führer will relieve you.'

Dietrich nodded gloomily. 'I know, I know. No one is secure in his appointment if he fails the Führer – Adolf Hitler hasn't the tolerance he once had. But what do you suggest, Lehmann?'

'Well, sir, like you, I don't want to throw the Division in at the deep end. We'll have to take risks, there's no avoiding that now. But we don't have to take *that* much of a risk.'

Dietrich grunted impatiently. 'Get on with it, Lehmann, piss or get off the pot! What do you mean?'

Lehmann flushed a little at Dietrich's crudity; the General really ought to put his days as an NCO behind him. 'We should hedge our bets. Send in perhaps a battalion to feel out the position and at the same time have another look at the place – this time, much more carefully.'

'How do you mean?' Dietrich was clutching at straws.

'Light aircraft, sir.'

Dietrich's face fell. 'Sorry, Lehmann – out of the question. Since Fat Hermann lost that Fieseler Storch, he's not giving the Bodyguard the dirt under his well-manicured nails.'

Lehmann smiled coldly. 'Champers,' he said.

'*Champers?*'

'Yes, sir – Peiper's reconnaissance battalion captured a whole depot full of the stuff this morning, real red Crimean champagne. You could have the whole of von Richthofen's Air Fleet for that kind of sauce.'

Dietrich beamed at his chief of staff. 'Of course, of course!' he said enthusiastically. 'Those fly-boys bathe in bubbly! They love the fizzy stuff. Go on, tell me more.'

'Well, sir, this is what I suggest. We send Peiper's battalion forward to recce the Miropol Position, and in advance of him, we'll have a low-flying aircraft.' He stopped abruptly, as was his wont. 'What do you think, sir?'

Dietrich slapped him across the back. '*Grossartig*, Lehmann!' he exclaimed delightedly. 'You don't know it, but you've just won yourself the scrambled egg for gallantry in action.' He beamed at the other man.

Now Lehmann's face lit up too. That meant Dietrich was going to ensure he received the German Cross in Gold, known in SS slang as the 'scrambled egg'. 'Thank you, Standartenführer. Then the plan stands?'

'Stand it does, Lehmann. Peiper won't like it, I know. He's devoted to his battalion.' Dietrich shrugged. 'But you can't make an omelette, without cracking eggs. Better Peiper's battalion than the whole division, what?'

Lehmann nodded in agreement. 'I suggest further, sir, that we set up a top-level radio link with him and the recce plane. As soon as we know exactly what the situation is on that height at Miropol, we follow up with the whole division. What do you think, sir?'

Dietrich considered for a moment, then said: 'Yes, let's do it like that. I've had enough of that Yid von Manstein breathing down my neck. Get Peiper over here – at the double!'

As Dietrich had anticipated, Peiper didn't like his new assignment. His thin handsome face set into a frown of displeasure when he heard the news: 'I have your permission to register a formal protest, sir?'

Dietrich caught himself just in time. 'You have my permission. Protest as much as you like, Peiper . . . But listen, it's not that bad, you know. You've got the fly-boy with his radio link. He'll keep you – and us – in the picture. If there really is something to worry about at Miropol, he'll let you know, and you can be sure I won't order you into action if the odds are against you.'

Dietrich's words had no effect on Peiper. His face set as before, he said, 'I rather doubt, sir, if you'll be the one who'll decide my actions for me when the crunch comes.'

'What do you mean, Peiper?'

'The Ivans, sir. They're the ones who are going to do the deciding at Miropol. Now, if you will excuse me?' Peiper clicked to attention and saluted.

Instinctively Dietrich touched his cap in acknowledgement and watched as the skinny young battalion commander jumped on the turret of his armoured car, waving his arm around three times, the signal for his drivers to start up. 'You know, Lehmann?' he cried above the roar of motors, 'I think that young Berlin shit just insulted me.' He looked at his chief of staff in surprise. 'I really do . . .'

SEVEN

The 'champers bomber' – as the men of Peiper's reconnaissance battalion called the little plane – 'rented' from the Luftwaffe – came winging in low above the long column, its engine throttled back almost to stalling speed.

'Stand by – message!' called Peiper in the lead car.

One of the crew poised on the dust-covered deck.

The pilot rocked his wing to left and right and then, leaning over the side of the cockpit, threw something out. There was a small white burst of silk, then a little parachute opened and a message started to sail down to earth. Even before the leading scout car had rolled to a halt, the crewman had sprung over the side and had grabbed the message as it came to rest on the baked steppe.

Hastily, Peiper pushed his dust goggles to the back of his black forage cap, decorated with the white skull-and-crossbones of the SS, and read the pencilled message. '*Cavalry rapidly approaching from east . . . estimated distance from your present position six kilometres . . . Good hunting.*'

Peiper dropped the message. 'Good hunting!' he muttered to himself, reaching for the binoculars hanging from his neck. 'What does that fly-boy think we are? A shitting fox-hunting club?'

While the radio-operator tensed over his apparatus, Peiper swept the horizon to the east with the glasses, blinking at the intense glare as the sun struck the calibrated glass. Now that the scout-car was no longer moving, Peiper could feel the sweat beginning to trickle down his dusty face amid the terrible heat. Behind him, the long column came to a halt, the gunners instinctively swinging their machine-guns and 37mm cannon round to point in the direction in which their chief was staring. Then he spotted them.

The whole burning ridge at ten o'clock was suddenly packed tight with dark figures on horseback. Only moments before the low hill had been bare of anything save brown gorse and yellow steppe grass; now it was covered with them, hundreds of them – perhaps thousands, for all he knew.

Peiper whistled softly and hurriedly focussed the glasses. Now he could see them more clearly as they lined up, gleaming sabres resting on their right shoulders, banners hanging limply down on the shoulders of the flag-bearers; here and there an officer trotted leisurely along their massed ranks, as if ensuring that his men's dressing was correct.

Next to Peiper, his adjutant Heinze let out a low whistle. 'In God's name, Hauptsturm, it's like something out of 1870[1]!'

Peiper said nothing, but his lean jaw clenched, as if he were suddenly angry at something or someone.

Now the silence along the long column was broken only by the soft throb of the engines, as the rest of the reconnaisance battalion watched the strange spectacle on the ridge in dumb awe.

The sun beat down unmercifully. Peering through his binoculars, and feeling the sweat trickle unpleasantly down the small of his back Peiper observed a tall, burly figure mounted on a pure white horse push his way through the massed ranks to the head of the cavalry. Behind him came another rider, bearing what looked like a bugle. On both sides the flag-bearers fell in and waited.

Peiper groaned, '*Not that!*'

'What, sir?' his adjutant asked hastily, and there was a note of panic in his voice. Like most of the men, he found there was something eerie in the way the Russians were

[1] Date of the Franco–Prussian War.

lining up on the ridge, so silent, so motionless – so threatening.

Peiper lowered his glasses, and swung round on the waiting radio-operator. Ignoring his suddenly white-faced adjutant, he cried, 'Signal the battalion to prepare for a charge!'

'*What, sir!*' the radio operator quavered, as if he could hardly believe his ears. 'What did you say, sir?'

'You heard me!' Peiper thundered. 'Do you want me to write it out in triplicate? The battalion is to prepare for a cavalry charge!'

'But Hauptsturm,' his adjutant yelled, above the sudden crackle of the air waves as the crimson-faced operator started rapping out his urgent message. 'You can't be serious! This is 1941, not 1871—'

He broke off suddenly. On the ridge the riders had begun to move.

Peiper dropped his glasses to his skinny chest and puffed out his cheeks in sudden resignation. 'Tell that to those gallant fools over there. Tell *them* that!' Then slowly, it seemed reluctantly, he swung himself behind the deck machine-gun, automatically checked to see if it was set to 'automatic', then settled down to wait in glum, brooding silence.

The Russians seemed to be advancing in a solid wall, the dust muffling the sound of their horses' hooves so that they moved silently, as if they were floating over the surface of the burning steppe. Now they were perhaps two kilometres away, and as the awed SS troopers watched their uncanny approach, they noted how each flank of the long column of horsemen started to curve inwards, so as to present a crescent formation of men and mounts, with its centre furthest away from the waiting defenders.

Peiper saw the manoeuvre too and remembered the tactic from those long, boring lectures the old tactics teacher had given at Bad Toelz long before the war. It wouldn't help the Russians. They couldn't hope to outflank him with his 37mm cannon and his machine-guns. The Popovs hadn't a chance. They were about to commit mass suicide.

Now they were a kilometre away, and the watchers could see them more clearly: big men, sabres resting on their right shoulders, trotting forward easily, the mild breeze furling out the big red banners of the flag-bearers; the sun gleamed brilliantly on the raised bugle of the trumpeter, who rode just behind the man on the white mount.

Peiper's adjutant groped for his canteen and without taking his awed gaze off the strange spectacle, took a hasty gulp of the luke-warm water. Peiper could hear it trickle down the man's parched throat and for some reason the sound made him angry; everything made him angry at this moment; for he knew what was going to happen next would not be war, but murder. 'Observe water discipline, Heinze, for God's sake! Drink when you're told to drink!'

'Sorry, sir . . . sorry, I forgot,' Heinze stuttered. 'It's this damned tension. I can't—'

He broke off suddenly.

The silver note of a bugle had come floating across the plain. Peiper gasped. The pace of the horsemen had changed. The trot had given way to a canter. Now the swirling cloud of baking white dust seemed to reach up and envelop the sweat-glazed bellies of the horses, and the banners began to stream out bravely, flapping in the wind.

Frantically Peiper wracked his brains to remember what that old instructor had told the bored young cadets about cavalry attacks. When exactly did they attack? At what distance? He recalled that the trot was followed by the canter – but for God's sake when did the canter give way to the gallop? *When*?

Now they were less than five hundred metres away. Now the air was full of the thunder of those massed hooves. Now their whole front seemed filled with men on horses. Everywhere the SS troopers waiting behind their guns, swallowed hard, eyes wide with horror, abruptly no longer so confident that they could stop this moving wall of men. They looked so purposeful, so confident, so invincible.

Peiper heard himself calling, 'Operator, signal – stand by to fire!'

'Stand by to fire!' the operator yelled back in a broken voice, as if any moment he might begin to scream hysterically.

Everywhere, the gunners wiped their sweating palms on the seat of their pants and grasped their triggers, knowing that their very lives depended on those little pieces of metal. Instantly their fingers were wet with sweat again.

Now the horsemen were two hundred metres away. Crouching over the machine-gun sights, Peiper aimed at the centre and the command group around the big man on the white mount. He was an old man with great, sweeping, old-fashioned cavalryman's moustaches; Peiper could not help thinking there was something terribly sad about his brown-wrinkled, weather-beaten face – as if he knew what the outcome of this attack would be, yet realized the inevitability of it.

Peiper gasped. The old man had raised his sabre. It gleamed silver in the sun. The bugler thrust his trumpet to his lips and blew a swift blast on it.

'*Urrah!*' Peiper felt a chill of fear sweep down his spine as that great Russian cry rose from hundreds of throats. In an instant the cavalry had broken into a furious gallop, the plain itself seemed to be trembling under the racing hooves, as the riders brought their sabres down, leaning low over the flying manes of their horses, charging forward, jostling with each other for position, their faces suddenly crazed with excitement.

'*Here they come!*' someone screamed. '*It's the charge!*'

'Don't shoot at the horses!' Peiper cried desperately, as his column opened fire.

But already it was too late. Carried away by fear and the almost unbearable tension, his troopers fired point-blank into the mass of men and mounts, hitting both riders and horses. Suddenly they were going down everywhere in a confused mêlée, screeching and screaming, hooves flailing the air, the dust erupting in thick clouds as they smashed to the ground, crushing their riders, trampling on them with their hooves, writhing in their death agonies.

Like the rest of his men, Peiper was carried away by the sudden ecstasy of fear and tension. He swung the machine-gun from left to right, pumping out slugs at 800 a minute, ripping them into the wave of cavalry that reared up above him and threatened to swamp him at any moment. A horse seemed to be about to spring right into the scout car. At ten metres' range he caught it, just as horse and rider launched forth into the air. Its soft belly exploded, a cascade of grey, pulsating entrails sloshed to the ground, and the animal went down, writhing back and forth and entangling itself in its own steaming guts, until a lucky grenade blew its head off. Its rider, killed outright, lay flat, arms outstretched like Christ on the Cross, on the glacis plate of the scout car, fiery-red blood streaming from every shattered limb.

Now an old man, his bald head scored with old sabre cuts, suddenly loomed up out of the confused mêlée in front of Peiper. Blood streaming down the side of his weathered face, he lunged with his sabre. It was the cavalry commander.

'No!' Peiper screamed. 'Don't make me . . . *no!*' He ducked and heard, rather than saw, the razor-sharp blade strike the glowing steel of his machine-gun barrel. The old man cursed thickly and lunged again, this time not so powerfully. Again Peiper dodged, and the blow went wide. Peiper dropped his grip on the machine-gun. The old man staggered back and forth below him, dying on his feet. Peiper could see that one whole side of him was black with blood. But he was determined to die with his decimated regiment – instinctively Peiper knew that. But *he* wouldn't be the one who'd kill him. Vainly the old man swung his silver sabre once more, his knees buckling slowly but surely beneath him like those of a boxer about to go down for the final count. Peiper ducked, hearing the sharp blade hiss through the air above his head. The old man groaned, and in that same instant Heinze blasted a burst of pistol bullets straight into his dying face at one metre's range. It burst apart in a flurry of bright scarlet, and Peiper felt the back of his bent head suddenly hot and wet with blood as the faceless old cavalry commander fell dead at last. Then he vomited.

A lone shell-shocked horse was zig-zagging crazily through the landscape of horror, dragging its dead rider by one stirrup behind it, thundering over the corpses of dead Russians and their mounts which littered the steppe like bundles of abandoned rags. It smashed into a tree. The impact shook the dead rider free at last, and the animal galloped away into the distance. Now the plain fell silent, abandoned to the dead and the awed, shocked watchers who remained motionless beside their steaming machine-guns and cannon. A heavy stillness descended on the steppe, broken only by the hum of the fat, blue-black flies which now began to descend greedily in their thousands on their juicy prey.

It seemed an age before Peiper became aware of the drone of the little spotter plane and realized that the signal flare which curved flatly across the dead plain, bathing the grotesque scene below in its eerie red light, was intended for him.

Slowly, very slowly, as if it were on rusty springs, he raised his head and stared at the plane circling above the battlefield, his eyes blank and seemingly unable to take in what was happening. At last he understood what the little flashes of icy light indicated. 'Signaller,' he commanded in a dead voice, 'read it.'

The signaller took his gaze off a dead Russian with a

gigantic gory hole bored into his chest by an unexploded 37mm shell, and wiped the back of his hand across his cracked lips. Shading his eyes against the last slanting rays of the sun, he started to read the morse. '*Route Z clear . . . No apparent enemy defence . . . Miropol Position shrouded in smoke . . . Unable to recce at any length . . . Seems clear though . . . Will pick you up at dawn tomorrow . . . back to base now . . . Schlaf schön . . . träume süess*[2] *. . . Out!*'

With that the light went out and the little plane curved hurriedly westwards, heading back for base, as if eager to get away from the eerie scene of death. Peiper was still too dumb from the slaughter of the Soviet cavalry to take offence at the pilot's last wish and his hasty retreat. Instead, with no emotion apparent in his voice, he said: 'Alright, Heinze, roll them again!'

Minutes later the column was disappearing into the growing darkness, and the battlefield was left to the slowly stiffening dead. But unknown to Peiper, his departure was being carefully observed, for hidden in the long parched grass, their nostrils heavy with the scent of spilled blood, sweet, pervasive and sickly, their faces coated with the hot dust of the steppe, lay other watchers.

A light wind sprang up, but still those watchers hidden in that glowing incandescence didn't move. They, too, might well have been as dead as the corpses all around them, sprawled in the grotesque attitudes of those whose lives have ended violently: then, finally, when the last sound of the engines had died away in the east, a vast shape arose and shook a fist at the departing Germans.

'*Revenge!*' Olga swore, her huge body trembling with suppressed rage. '*Revenge!*'

As she stared around at the piles of dead, her comrades passed among the bodies like grey ghosts, haggard faces begrimed with dirt, contorted with sorrow and anger at

[2] Sleep well . . . sweet dreams.

what they had witnessed that terrible afternoon. 'It was them,' she said in a hushed voice, looking down at the dead boy at her feet, his legs tucked oddly beneath his shattered body, but with his cap still set on his blond curls at the jaunty angle of the typical cavalryman. 'The killers of Hitler's own Bodyguard. And now we know where they are going – *to Miropol!*'

She waved her hand. In silent obedience, the women of the Partisan Guards started to trail after her towards Miropol.

EIGHT

Otto dozed in the corner of the gloomy bunker, oblivious to the steady *rat-tat* of the Soviet machine-gunner, who was firing routine bursts at the thick concrete walls of their refuge. In his dream he was making a speech somewhere in a great open space – somewhere green and lush. 'The sin,' he was telling his vast, faceless audience, who were listening in awed, impressed silence, 'is to believe you can buy your luck. Because you can't! Take me, for example—' here he struck his chest, '—I've always regarded myself as a particularly lucky bastard—' there was a chuckle of laughter from his audience at the great man's mild profanity '—up to now. But am I? I ask you – *am I?* I'm a German, so that's one black mark against me for a start. I'm hitched up with a mad fool called Count von der Weide, so that's another black—'

'—Otto.' An urgent voice cut into his great speech and someone started to shake his shoulder.

Otto groaned and kept his eyes tightly closed.

'*Otto!*' the Count persisted. 'Wake up at once! *Please!*'

Still keeping his eyes closed, Otto muttered, 'Where's the blonde maid with the short skirt and the frilly French drawers serving morning coffee? That reminds me, my cock has been in mothballs for about a hundred years, I could do with a little bit of the old mattress pol—'

'Otto!' The count cut him short with unaccustomed firmness. 'Open your eyes and stop talking rubbish!'

Otto did as he was told and stared up at the Count's unshaven, anxious face. 'What is it?'

By way of answer, the Count beckoned him over to the

main periscope of the bunker, housed just behind the tremendous cannon. 'Take a look up there – at ten o'clock.'

Otto rubbed the back of his hand across his scummed lips – there was little water in the bunker and they were rationing themselves.

'To your left,' continued the Count. 'Look a little upwards. It should still be there . . .'

Otto did as he was commanded, and adjusting the metal knob, raised the gleaming circle of calibrated glass so as to point over the immediate front of the Miropol Position and straight ahead into the dawn sky.

Almost immediately a small black shape came into view; and as the plane wheeled to the right, the rays of the new sun glinted on the glass of its cockpit.

'It's one of ours,' cried Otto, suddenly excited. 'I can see the swastika quite clearly on its tail! Heaven, arse and cloudbust, I never thought I'd ever be so glad to welcome that damned thing!' He swung round on the Count. 'Our boys are on the way, Count! We're saved! They'll pull our hooters out of the crap for us! It's one of our spotter planes.'

But the Count seemed not to be infected by Otto's sudden enthusiasm. Instead he said gloomily, 'Possibly, Otto. But before they do manage to – er – pull our hooters out of the crap, as you put it in your charming working-class way, they're going to be in for a very bad beating.'

Otto's smile vanished. 'What do you mean?'

'Take a look at number five turret.'

Obediently Otto swung the periscope round above the heads of the infantry dug in all around their own bunker, and focused it on the bunker with the sole remaining effective cannon. Russians were hurrying back and forth, lugging great wads of gun-cotton, shoulders bent under heavy artillery shells, while the gun itself was being raised skywards so that its muzzle was now pointing up at a thirty-degree angle.

'The other three are doing the same,' the Count said gloomily. 'I checked before I woke you. Of course, they won't be able to fire. But Number Five will be – and just one of those monsters can do a tremendous amount of damage.'

Otto relinquished his hold on the periscope and faced the Count, who sat slumped dejectedly on a box of rations next to the breech of the cannon. 'You mean to the Bodyguard?'

'Yes. That spotter plane means they're within range. That's why the Russians spread the smoke screen yesterday . . . They're preparing to fire.'

Otto bit his bottom lip, his brain racing, desperately trying to find some sort of solution to their problem. 'Listen,' he said urgently, 'couldn't we try to knock out Number Five with our own pea-shooter here?' He slapped the massive steel breech. 'You seem to know something about these monsters and I could help you.'

The Count shook his head sadly. 'I've already considered that possibility, Otto. But it won't work.'

'Why?'

'Because this bunker is a fixed position with a traverse of about thirty degrees. Number Five is some ten or fifteen degrees beyond our traverse. Besides, even if we could swing the cannon around to that area, we couldn't lower the cannon far enough to hit Number Five. No, that's out.'

Again Otto thought of all those eager young faces he had seen in training back in Rumania. Blind National Socialist fools as they were, he couldn't just let them be slaughtered like this. 'But there must be some way, Count,' he said desperately, his eyes roaming round the gloomy, littered interior of the bunker. 'We've succeeded in putting four of the big bastards out of action. There's only that one shit left.' He slammed his fist angrily into the open palm of his left hand. '*There must be a way!*'

Sadly the Count shook his head. 'Don't think, Otto, that I haven't wracked my brains for an answer. But—' he shrugged hopelessly '—there just isn't one.' He gave a sigh and added with a note of finality. 'The Bodyguard will just have to take its punishment . . .'

At nine o'clock precisely that morning, the *rat-tat* of machine-gun fire against the thick walls of their bunker suddenly ceased. Immediately Otto and the Count roused themselves from their gloomy reverie and sprang to the left and right periscopes. Again a smoke screen was beginning to submerge the Miropol Position in a thick white cloud, as it had done the day before. But it was not yet thick enough to conceal the figures hurrying into the bunkers and the men grouped around the great range-finder which had been set up in the centre of the bunker-line.

The Count read Otto's thoughts. 'Yes,' he said, 'they're going to open fire. Our people are out there somewhere – and now they're within range.'

Otto swallowed hard and focused his periscope on the first three bunkers, their monstrous guns already raised skywards. He could just visualize the half-naked gunners poised behind their death-dealing weapons, while the gunnery officers counted off the seconds, eyes glued to the green-glowing dials of their watches. With every moment, the unsuspecting Germans of the Leibstandarte were drawing closer, driving right into the terrible trap which had been laid for them.

There was a hoarse command from the group of men half crouched around the big range-finder. An officer straightened up, a dark, half-visible silhouette now in the swirling white smoke that had begun to envelop him. He raised his hand expectantly, body turned towards the pillboxes.

'It's a matter of moments now, Otto,' the Count's anxious voice cut into the tense silence of their own bunker. 'When he brings down—'

The Count never finished his sentence. The officer's hand flashed down and cut him off in mid-sentence.

From the first three bunkers there came muffled cries of anger, curses, shouts, commands and counter-commands. Men started to stream out into the open, milling around, shaking their heads, bellowing at each other. '*Sabotja!*' Someone screamed. Obviously they had discovered what the Count had done to their weapons. But Otto had no eyes for them now; his gaze was fixed almost hypnotically on Number Five, as its long, sinister black barrel rose into the white swirling fog, like the snout of some primeval monster sniffing the air for the first scent of its unsuspecting prey. He caught his breath. It could only be seconds now.

There was a kind of huge sigh, followed an instant later by an earth-shaking roar. Otto held on to the periscope for dear life as the bunker trembled like a ship at sea struck by a sudden tornado. The glass of the periscope filled with flame – yellow, red, purple – replaced almost the next moment by a massive thrust of black, billowing smoke. With a great angry baleful scream, the first half-hundred-weight shell went hurtling into the air. Otto reeled back, shocked to the very bone. The destruction of the Bodyguard had commenced . . .

Peiper, leading a column of armoured cars and half-tracks which was strung out in a long line across the steppe, was first to hear that strange red-hot sighing, followed by the grating squeak that a diamond makes when it is drawn hard across glass. He turned suddenly, his handsome face set in a puzzled frown. Next to him Heinze heard it too.

'What in three devils' name is—'

The rest of his words were drowned by the roar of a single great shell, plunging straight down from the burning blue morning sky. With a mighty antiphonal crash it smashed right into the centre of the column. A half-track leapt into the air in a crazy dance, panzer grenadiers tumbling from it, arms and legs flailing like toy soldiers. Fifty metres away an armoured reconnaissance car was lifted straight upwards as if by an invisible hand. Next instant it hit the ground again and disintegrated.

'God almighty!' Peiper cried, his thin face suddenly ashen with shock. 'What was that?'

The thunder of the next shell as it plunged to earth, ripping a huge steaming hole in the steppe and burying two armoured cars in churned soil, gave him his answer. '*Heavy artillery!*' he cried above the earth-shaking roar, as yet another shell came ripping through the sky, tearing the very air out of his lungs with its impact and making him gasp and stutter, fighting desperately for air like a drowning man. '*Disperse . . . Disperse!*'

Suddenly it was every man for himself. The full fury of that man-made cyclone swamped the column and the air was filled with the thunderously amplified staccato of the shell-storm, drowning the very world in a terrible, seemingly never-ending barrage.

But end it finally did. Peiper, cowering face-downwards on the earth next to the burning wreck of his command car, surrounded by the massacred bodies of his crew, ripped the ground with his bleeding fingernails, his whole body trembling uncontrollably. His ears were still filled with that terrible roaring and he was unable to believe that his terrible ordeal was over. How long he lay like that, sobbing like a heart-broken child, his body twitching at every limb, soaked in his own urine, he never could recall. Perhaps it was only five minutes; but to him it seemed an eternity before he finally dared to raise his head, feeling the clods of earth and pieces of shrapnel roll from his helmet. For minutes all he could do was stare with wide-eyed wonder at the hideously transformed lunar landscape which now presented itself to him.

His battalion had been virtually destroyed by that tremendous barrage. Destroyed, damaged, burning half-tracks and scout cars lay everywhere, tossed to one side like children's toys by those terrible shells; the remains of the men they had once contained were scattered among the steaming holes or flung into the trees, where they hung now like grisly human birds.

His eyes filled with horror, Peiper staggered to his feet and watched as the other survivors did the same, rising out of the folds in the ground where they had hidden like ashen ghosts, unable to speak, hobbling towards their commander, tears rolling down their cheeks, hands held out in front of them like blind men feeling their way.

Peiper shook his head hard like a man trying to wake from a heavy sleep and looked around for an intact vehicle with a radio. There weren't many of them left. Then he spotted a half-track, its engine still running, with the gleam of a wireless aerial appearing through the slowly clearing clouds of smoke.

On legs that felt as if they were made of rubber and which threatened to give way underneath him at any moment, he started for it. He had to report to Dietrich; *he had to!* As he walked, avoiding the looks of the survivors, he formulated his message for the Old Man. It would be brutal in its simplicity. '*Reconaissance Battalion Peiper wiped out . . . Drive on the Miropol Position ended as of now . . .*'

NINE

Otto's plan first began to take shape while he was poking moodily around the interior of the bunker, trying to forget the terrible barrage and the casualties it must have inflicted on the Leibstandarte. 'Any idea what this is, Count?' he asked, indicating a short metal tube with a five-pronged fork protruding from the muzzle.

The Count, who was gloomily chewing on a mouldy apple which he had found among the Russian soldiers' pathetic rations, looked up. 'It's a mortar grapnel, Otto,' he replied. 'The tube contains a small explosive charge. When it's fired' – he paused a moment as yet another burst of Russian fire whacked against the concrete wall of the bunker '—the rope attached to the grapnel you can see shoots right up the side of a cliff or whatever it is that has to be scaled.'

'Cliff-scaling – what for?'

The Count shrugged sadly; he, too, was still depressed by the thought of the damage that the great gun some fifty metres away must have done this morning. 'Infantry sometimes have to scale cliffs in an assault attack and they need the support of the artillery and engineers to get them up as quickly and as safely as possible.'

'I see,' Otto said and fell silent again.

It was some time later, when the Russian machine-gun fire had finally ceased, probably while the gunners took a nap in the scorching afternoon sun, that Otto said carefully, 'You know, of course, Count, that there's no way out of this place? They're watching both the back and side entrances, just like the old bailiffs used to watch my mother, the Witch's place when they thought she was going to do one of her moonlight flits.'

The Count, resting on a pile of sacks, hands beneath his head, looked at his friend. 'You're thinking, Otto, aren't you?' he said slowly. 'I can see it in your eyes, my young friend. You're on to something.' He half rose.

Otto held out both hands, as if to push him away. 'Hold your water, Count,' he said hastily. '*So schnell schiessen die Preussen nicht!*[1] Let me ask *you* a question first.'

'Fire away.'

'The distance between Bunker Four and Bunker Five is about fifty metres, right?'

The Count nodded his agreement.

'Now this grapnel thing – what length of rope does it carry, do you reckon?'

The Count swung himself up, crossed to the grapnel mortar and held his arm against it. 'I estimate one length of rope is the length of my arm, so that should make it – say – fifty centimetres. There are,' he made a quick calculation, 'one hundred and – er – twenty lengths of rope in the container. So we've got about sixty metres of rope attached to the grapnel.'

'Ten metres to spare, perhaps,' Otto said, sucking his front teeth thoughtfully.

The Count could contain himself no longer. 'What's in your mind, Otto?'

'This. We can't get out of this place to attack Number Five – at least, not unless we want a nice lead sandwich from the Popovs waiting for us outside. So what's left?' He answered his own question. 'Either we dig our way out – which is out of the question – or,' he pointed upwards, 'we can fly from here.'

'*Fly?*'

'Yes. See that?' He indicated the dark square hole in the ceiling, just above the breech of the big gun.

'Yes.'

[1] A German saying: 'The Prussians don't shoot that fast.'

Well, I think I could just about squeeze myself into it. I imagine it's some sort of ventilation shaft, eh?'

'Exactly. When a cannon of this calibre fires, Otto, a great deal of toxic gas is released. I've noticed the Russians don't have any kind of extractor fan, so my guess is that that hole is used to extract the main propellant gases once the breech is opened.'

Otto absorbed the information. 'Have you any idea of how that shaft might run, Count?'

'Well, obviously they wouldn't want anybody climbing in through it or being able to fire or use a flame-thrower down it, so I expect it'll be angled-off somehow – it's the usual technique. Then it'll lead up to some sort of grating.'

'The roof's covered with earth as camouflage, Count,' Otto reminded the other man hastily.

'Oh yes, of course. Perhaps there won't be a grating, then. But,' the Count could contain his curiosity no longer, 'what is your plan, *please*?'

Otto hesitated only a fraction of a second, knowing that if and when he spoke he would be committing himself to a course of action that might well result in Mrs Stahl's handsome son ending up by looking at potatoes from below two metres of earth. 'Count,' he announced with an air of finality, 'I'm going to use that shaft up there to knock out Number Five.'

The Count gasped, but Otto didn't give him time to speak. Instead he said simply, 'Tonight . . .'

Otto wasn't the only one that afternoon planning for the coming night. Some twenty kilometres away, an angry Jochen Peiper, recovered now from the decimation of his Battalion, squatted in the cover of a small wood with the survivors, chewing solidly on a piece of hard salami while he took stock of his position.

Thirty minutes before he had been called to the only intact radio by the signaller. Sepp Dietrich was on the other end. Dietrich had wasted no time in commiserating with him on the tragic fate of his Battalion; instead, he had got down to business in his customary bull-at-a-gate manner. 'I'm sending up Panzermeyer's panzer grenadiers, Peiper,' he had announced briskly, 'plus two flame-thrower teams under Sergeant Major Hartung. As soon as they reach you, you're to move off. Speed march, your recce people leading the way. You should be in position and ready to attack at dawn.'

Peiper groaned audibly. 'But General,' he had protested, 'it'll be no use. That gun will slaughter us. I've never seen or heard anything like it before. Even back in '40 at the Maginot Line, the Frogs never had a popgun like that.'

Dietrich had overruled his objection. 'You'll move under cover of darkness' he had barked. 'That should do the trick, don't you think, Peiper?'

'No, I don't sir,' he had snapped back. 'The Popovs are out there everywhere. From where I'm standing now,' he had squinted his eyes against the rays of the setting sun, and peered at the dark shapes of the horsemen on the horizon, 'I can see at least six Ivan scouts. They're watching our every move. As soon as they report that we're moving off again, I don't doubt that that monstrous weapon will start ranging in on us again.'

Dietrich had laughed, though Peiper sensed there was no conviction in the laughter. 'Now come on, Jochen, you were never one to throw your rifle into the corn.[2] Everyone knows the Ivans can't shoot straight to save their lives. String the column out as much as possible, move fast and dig in on dead ground as soon as you arrive at the Miropol Position. Believe me, it's simply a matter of boldness and surprise. You'll be doing something the Ivans won't be expecting you to do!'

Peiper cleared his throat and made a final attempt at protest. 'Cover twenty kilometres in the dark with no knowledge of the terrain to speak of; run the risk of our

[2] German expression for giving up.

armoured vehicles being knocked out by some half-arsed Popov armed with an anti-tank rifle; dig in positions presumably held by Russian infantry defending the Miropol Position and hope to do all that before those damned gunners spot we've moved!' Peiper exploded. 'Sir, the whole plan stinks! It's sheer suicide. Panzermeyer's battalion will suffer the same fate as mine.'

There was a note of pleading in Dietrich's voice when he spoke again. 'Listen Jochen, don't make waves, *please*! I understand your position, believe me I do. I know your feeling for your men. But understand my position, too. They're all breathing fire down my neck – von Manstein, Keitel, and now the Führer. I take the Miropol Position, or I go.' At the other end Peiper heard Dietrich force a note of warmth into his strained voice. 'Remember, we're the Bodyguard, Jochen, and you're one of the best of my younger officers; you've a great career in front of you once this campaign is over, believe you me. Don't think or feel too much – it's fatal. I learned that in the First War. Go at 'em like Blücher and hit them over the head with a sockful of shit! That's the only way to do it.'

Peiper had groaned to himself. It was typical of Dietrich and his kind; they thought a crudity of that kind would solve all problems. Don't think, just fight. 'All right, sir,' he had said icily. 'I'll do as you suggest. But here and now I'd like to register a formal protest against this course of action.'

Peiper heard the relief in Dietrich's voice quite clearly. 'Register all the protests you like, my dear Jochen,' he had exclaimed happily. 'But get to Miropol by dawn!'

Now, as he squatted in the wood with his silent men, listening to the first soft rustle of the night wind in the dry grass of the steppe, his nostrils assailed by the sweet dry scent of the baked dust, Peiper was wondering how he should go about it. In his heart he knew he was committing what was left of his own Battalion and probably Panzermeyer's too to death. He personally wasn't afraid to die;

but his men – that was something else. He glanced around
at them, their faces still pale and strained from the ordeal
of that morning, each man slumped in weary introspection.
How young they looked. Apart from the handful of
surviving NCOs, most of them were hardly out of their
teens. Probably most of them virgins too. And here he
was, being asked to sacrifice their young lives. Peiper
clenched his fists with suppressed rage until his nails dug
into his palms painfully. It was a damnable decision he had
to make. Still he made it. He wouldn't wait for Panzermeyer
and his grenadiers. Together they would make too tempting
a target for that monstrous gun over there to the east.
Perhaps he could go it alone? Perhaps the Popovs wouldn't
open fire on the handful of men and vehicles which were
all he had left? Perhaps he might be lucky and make it
before dawn?

Perhaps? a cynical little voice in the back of his brain
sneered. *Perhaps?* He dismissed the voice. Tossing away
the stump of salami, he rose to his feet, animated by new
energy. 'NCOs,' he called, breaking the heavy brooding
silence, 'get your sections together!' The men looked round
at him, startled. 'Los, los,' he cried, clapping his hands
together like an irate schoolteacher at a bunch of slow
pupils. '*Dalli . . . dalli!* Get some pepper in yer pants!'

Hastily the NCOs sprang to their feet, grabbing for their
helmets and repeating the cries.

'Night march!' Peiper commanded. '*Mount up!*'

Ten minutes later, what was left of Reconnaissance
Battalion Peiper was trundling eastwards once more into
the ever-lengthening shadows, while on the heights, the
Cossack signaller was rapping out the news on his ancient
morse-key . . .

Captain Shukov, Commander of Number Five turret,
waited impatiently as the operator wrote the final words
down on his message pad, the beads of sweat on his

forehead gleaming in the flickering light of the candle which was the bunker's sole illumination. All around him, his gunners, enjoying their evening ration of one hundred grams of vodka, tensed too. Perhaps this was another call to action.

Finally the operator was ready and the key ceased to click. Tearing off the message, he handed it to the dark-eyed officer, who in spite of his White-Russian name, had the great hooked nose of a Georgian. Hastily Shukov seized it and flashed his gaze along it, while his gunners waited, cups and canteens poised at their lips.

'*Fritzes on the move again* . . .' Shukov read out for their benefit, '*two scout cars and six half-tracks* . . . *estimated one hundred men in extended order* . . . *heading in a south-easterly direction* . . . *shadowing* . . .'

'They're coming for us, Comrade Captain,' said Kirov, a great bearded ruffian of a sergeant. 'The Fritz shitehawks haven't had enough!' Letting out a mighty guffaw, he slapped one of the great gleaming copper shell-cases at his side. 'It'd give me the greatest of pleasure to slip one of these beauties up their arseholes again – *without the vaseline!*'

The gunners, flushed with vodka and with the success of their morning shoot, joined in Kirov's laughter.

Shukov smiled and held up his hand for silence. 'Comrades, comrades, I have no doubt that Comrade Sergeant Kirov here would be very effective at that particular little task – though personally I prefer female gash to Fritz arseholes.' In high good humour the men laughed again, and Shukov beamed at them, thinking what good loyal fellows and excellent gunners they were. 'But I have a feeling here,' he touched his heart, 'that this might well be a feint. No commander in his right mind, not even a Fritz, would send a mere hundred men to attack the Miropol Position. Why, we've got at least three companies of infantry outside protecting the bunkers, not to mention the gunners in One, Two and Three! No – we're not going to waste our precious beauties,' he indicated the pile of shells heaped near the breech of the great cannon, 'on some Fascist feint.' His dark eyes narrowed and he stroked his beak-like nose in the Georgian fashion. 'There's something else coming our way – some nice, fat, juicy Fritz pigeon, which we're going to take apart in due course.'

'But what about *this* lot of Fritzes?' Kirov asked.

Shukov shrugged carelessly. 'Let the scouts or the partisans take care of them. A mere hundred men! We've got better things to do.' Carried away by sudden enthusiasm, Captain Shukov seized the jam-jar which contained his own ration of vodka. 'Comrades,' he cried, raising his glass, 'I'll give you a toast.'

'*A toast!*' their hoarse voices cried in unison, for like all Russians, the prospect of a toast always filled them with excitement.

'To the morrow – and the great slaughter of the Fascist beast!' he bellowed.

'*To the morrow and the great slaughter of the Fascist beast!*' they echoed.

As one, they drained their vodka and then, as if by some unspoken command, flung their canteens against the wall of the bunker, faces flushed with overweening confidence . . .

TEN

'Otto, my boy,' the Count said emotionally, taking Otto's hand in both of his, 'you will be careful, won't you?'

Though his mind was elsewhere, Otto flashed him a smile. 'Don't worry, Count. You know the old saying – you can't kill weeds.' *Famous last words*, a little voice inside him whispered. He ignored it and made a last check of his equipment.

Next to the ration crate on which he would step to reach the shaft, rested two Tommy-guns and the grapnel mortar, plus a handful of Russian stick-grenades and most important of all, the smoke bombs. With luck they'd do the trick, and he wouldn't be forced to kill his fellow human beings yet again.

Satisfied, he stepped up on the crate. 'All right, Count, this is it. Keep your fingers crossed for me.' So saying, he reached up and with a slight grunt, hauled himself into the shaft, feeling a gust of cooler air on the back of his head.

For a moment he crouched there, letting his eyes accustom themselves to the gloom; then, taking a deep breath, he commenced wriggling his way up the tight shaft, feeling the rope attached to his right ankle begin to play out behind him. Down below, the Count would now be holding it, for this was going to be their own personal umbilical cord.

Umbilical cord – the term shot through his brain. It was very apt. He did feel at this moment, as if he were back in the womb, struggling to make his way out. As his mother, the Witch, was wont to comment in her more sober moments, 'I always say, it went in easier than it came out!'

Forgetting the parallel, he wormed his way higher up the tight shaft, feeling the rough concrete scrape his knees painfully and graze the skin off his shoulders. His head hit something. For a moment he almost panicked. Was he trapped? Then he remembered the Count's remark that the shaft would be angled to prevent direct access to the bunker below. After a moment's struggle, suddenly he was moving again. The Count had been right. The shaft had moved to the right at a forty-five-degree angle.

Now the scent of dry earth met his nostrils. He pushed on eagerly. He was coming out of the damned shaft. The smell must come from the soil and vegetation camouflaging the roof. He felt a dry trickle of soil against the back of his neck. He could have given a shout of joy. He was there. He had almost done it. One final heave, and then he was out, sprawled flat on the cropped turf, his chest heaving wildly, as if he had just run a great race. *He had done it!*

For some time he lay there, sprawled full-length, taking in the little sounds of the night all around him: the cry of some forlorn bird, the soft wind in the trees, the lazy whisper of tired men, the clink of metal against metal – a reminder that there were dangerous armed men out there, no more than a matter of metres away, men who would shoot him down like a dog without hesitation.

Otto fought to control his breathing, and wiping the dry soil from his sweat-lathered face, began to crawl to the edge of the roof. He took his time, placing his hands and feet with great care; up here he was completely exposed, and at the mercy of any Ivan rifleman who spotted him.

He paused some sixty centimetres from the edge, and bringing his gaze down from below and working upwards – the old trick to obtain the best possible vision at night – he observed the scene to his front. The other bunker was clearly visible, outlined a squat, dark shape against the lighter hue of the night sky. Doing his best to block out the faint pink glare of the silent barrage which lit up the sky to the west, he tried to make out what kind of positions lay below him and between the two bunkers. Because if there were any, they were going to present the greatest danger to his bold plan.

He watched for what seemed to him an age and had just about satisfied himself that there were no Russians between the two bunkers, when down below someone scratched a match and in the spurt of blue flame he just had time to make out half-a-dozen helmeted soldiers grouped around what appeared to be a light machine-gun, dug in behind a pile of sandbags.

Abruptly the flame flickered out and he lay there blinking in the fresh darkness, cursing silently to himself. Not only was he going to have to risk his neck like some shitting acrobat, but he also was to run the risk of having his eggs shot off from below if he was spotted! It was all too much. For a moment his courage drained from him and he found himself trembling with fear. But in the end he pulled himself together and commenced the crawl back to the entrance to the shaft, where he tugged the rope three times – the signal he had agreed upon with the Count.

One moment later, the Count tugged the rope himself. The first item was ready. Carefully, very carefully, Otto started to haul it up, at the same time allowing the other end of the rope to descend back into the shaft, so that the Count could attach the next item. Pray God the Count had done the job properly, so the item wouldn't get caught at the angle halfway up the shaft!

The Count had worked well. Five minutes later, Otto was undoing the little sack containing the grenades and signalling the Count to proceed with item Number Two.

Again everything went off without a hitch, and as he placed one tommy-gun close to him, snapping off the safety-catch as he did so, Otto began to feel they had a chance of success. At least now, if the Popovs did spot him on the roof, he had some sort of muscle. Now all that was left to be brought up was the all-important mortar-grapnel.

The rope started to move again. Although they'd covered

both ends of the tube with sacking, it still made a faint noise as it scraped against the sides of the shaft, and Otto broke into a fresh sweat of fear as it came closer and closer; he knew just how far the slightest sound carried at night. If the Popovs down below spotted him now, the whole business would be over before it had even begun.

Nearer and nearer came the mortar. He could follow its slow progress up the shaft quite clearly. For the first time since he had been kicked out of Berlin-Wedding's *Volksschule*, Otto started to pray, willing the damned thing to come to the surface the very next instant.

Then it happened. The rope stopped moving through his hands. He waited a fleeting second and then tugged gently. Nothing happened. His brow was dripping with sweat now and he had to shake his head angrily to prevent the drops falling from his eyebrows and blinding him. He tugged again. Once more nothing. Then he realized what had happened. The damned thing had caught in the angle. For one long moment he lay there on his belly, rope in his hands, totally bewildered, completely unable to think what he should do next. Immobile, paralysed, stupid.

With an effort of sheer willpower, he pulled himself together. Desperately he made himself visualize how the shaft ran. Did the angle go to left or right from where he lay? What side could the damned tube have got caught on?

Licking his suddenly parched lips, he started to play out the rope gently again. There was a slight noise of metal striking stone. He guessed that the tube had gone down the shaft a little way again – somewhere below the angle.

His foot was tugged urgently. That would be the Count wondering what was going on. He ignored him. There was nothing the old boy could do just now. It was entirely up to him. The back of his shirt wet with sweat, a nerve in his left cheek suddenly ticking violently with the almost unbearable tension, hardly daring to breathe, Otto began to pull up the tube once more, playing it like some deep-sea angler trying to land a particularly pesky, deeply cunning catch.

A sudden noise below. He started. Then he guessed – that would be the tube hitting the angle in the shaft again. He swallowed hard. It was now or never. Exceedingly gingerly, feeling his heart beating like a trip-hammer under the strain, willing the damned thing not to get stuck this time, he edged it around the bend, millimetre by millimetre, telling himself that if he had guessed wrong and it got stuck again, he would break down and sob.

But now it seemed to be moving more swiftly – he could tell from the little noises that came from the shaft. An instant later the dark shape came clattering softly onto the roof of the bunker and Otto had collapsed flat on his face, all strength drained from his body, as weak as a new-born babe.

The attack came totally without warning. Just as Peiper had halted the column to make a more thorough check of his position, there came the nerve-shredding *brhhh-brhhh* of a tommy-gun only metres away. Peiper ducked hastily as a burst of gunfire stitched a line of holes the length of his half-track. Almost immediately, his own machine-guns started to hammer away all along the column. Hastily he swung up his own machine-pistol, his mind racing, every nerve tingling. Stabs of angry flame were cutting the darkness all around the halted column. Making a lightning calculation, he estimated he was being attacked by at least two companies.

Tracer from the cross-fire zipped through the darkness. He recognized the tactic. They were trying to pin the column down. But what was going to follow? An instant later he found out. There was the thwack, plop and obscene belch of a mortar being fired. Suddenly the air was ripped apart as three bombs exploded in quick succession some twenty metres away from the column, the shock waves slamming into the side of his own half-track and for one frightening moment, threatening to overturn it. '*Piss-poor shots!*' he cried above the racket, trying to reassure his startled men.

'What are they going to do now?' Heinze yelled.

'It's not what *they're* going to do,' Peiper yelled back, carried away once more by the old excitement of close combat, 'but what *we're* going to do!' Ignoring the slugs cutting the darkness everywhere and the hail of fist-sized, red-glowing mortar shrapnel, he stood upright and raised his flare pistol. He pressed the trigger. A soft plop. *Crack!* The star shell exploded immediately to his front, instantly bathing the steppe an icy, glowing, eerie silver.

'*They're there!*' a half-dozen excited voices screamed, as the rough skirmish line was surprised by the sudden light, their attackers suddenly halted and blinded by the intensity of the silver glow.

'*Fire!*' Peiper yelled, and dropping his flare pistol, ripped up his machine-pistol.

His men needed no encouragement. They pumped a vicious hail of fire into the skirmishers. Great gaps appeared in their ranks suddenly, as soldier after soldier went down, arms and legs flailing, screaming with sudden agony as lead tore into his body. And then almost as soon as it had started the surprise attack fizzled out and the survivors were running for cover, throwing away their weapons and jostling frantically with one another in their panic-stricken haste to get out of range.

'Cease fire,' Peiper yelled. 'Cease fire! Save your ammo . . . *Cease Fire* . . .'

The firing slowly began to die down, until finally, after one last furious burst fired into the writhing bodies lying a hundred metres to their front, it gave way altogether, and the short burst of frantic, crazed activity was followed by that strange quietness that always follows combat.

Peiper sat down suddenly. He was soaked in perspiration and he could hardly hold the machine-pistol in his trembling hands. Next to him, Heinze vaulted over the side of the truck and doubled swiftly towards the line of dead Russians sprawled out in the growing darkness, while the flare started to come down slowly like a fallen angel. Peiper saw him reach the first dead soldier, then turn, obviously shocked by what he saw.

'Hauptsturm . . . they're women – *real feminine women!*'

'Shit on the shingle,' Peiper's radio operator breathed, 'fancy wasting all that gash like that!'

But Peiper listened to neither Heinze nor the radio operator. His mind was elsewhere. Suddenly he was experiencing a surge of renewed hope. If the Russians risked casualties in such an amateurish and foolhardy attack, didn't it mean that they might not use that monstrous cannon against him? Even though they obviously knew his present position? Dietrich might be right after all. 'Go at 'em like Blücher and hit them over the head with a sockful of shit!' Perhaps that *was* the best tactic. Drive hard and take the Position by surprise. At least he had half a chance now. With renewed confidence, Peiper rose to his feet and interrupted the excited chatter of his men. 'All right, you cardboard soldiers, don't stand there waiting for the fart to hit the thunderbox! Roll 'em, now! Tempo! Tempo! *Come on, you lucky bastards, I've got a beautiful battle for you!*'

The faint snap and crackle of the firelight to the west roused Otto out of his self-induced lethargy and reminded him of the danger of his exposed position out here on the roof of the bunker. He could be spotted at any moment. He *had* to take his bold plan a stage further, however much he hated the idea.

He gave two tugs on the rope attached to his ankle – the signal for the Count to start playing his part in phase two of the operation. The Count replied with two tugs of his own. Somehow Otto could feel his old friend's concern. 'Sentimental old shit,' he said to himself. Hurriedly untying the rope, he began crawling forward to the edge of the roof, taking care to present as low a silhouette as possible in the faint yellow glow of the veiled moon. At the edge he waited, noting that the firing was dying away now and that the chatter below was ceasing, too. All that remained now was to count off the seconds till the Count went into action.

It began with a bang. Suddenly the first flare burst out of the frontal firing slot of the bunker and exploded just above the Russian positions below, colouring them a glowing red and leaving the terrain behind pitch black. The next instant, the Count pressed the trigger of the turret machine-guns, which were fired by remote control from below. Immediately they commenced spitting tracer at the surprised Russians.

They reacted immediately. Vicious streams of tracer started to curve their way towards the bunker. Whistles shrilled. Officers bellowed orders. Men ran from other bunkers, fumbling with their weapons. Wild, confused firing broke out on all sides.

Otto waited no longer. Thrusting up the grapnel-mortar at a forty-five-degree angle, he muttered a swift prayer, then turned the firing-knob as the Count had shown him. There was a sudden thwack. He felt the tube grow hot in his other hand. A wave of acrid blast slapped him in the face and forced him to close his eyes. An abrupt slithering noise. He opened his eyes. The rope was slithering out of the tube at a tremendous rate, shooting forward across the gap between the two bunkers. Again he prayed fervently, head cocked to one side so as to hear better.

Suddenly there was the clatter of metal against stone. Otto swallowed hard. Dare he try? He *had* to. Raising himself to his knees, he grasped the rope firmly in both hands and pulled hard. Nothing happened. The grapnel held. He jerked again to make sure, harder this time. It still held. Breathing a sigh of relief, he dabbed his forehead, which was wet with excited sweat.

Now he doubled back to the rear of the bunker, pulling the line with him. Swiftly he looped it around the exit to the shaft, pulled the loop tight and secured it with a snap hook. He tested it with his full weight. It hardly sagged. So far, so good. Then he busied himself hanging the weapons about his person, making sure that the smoke grenade was located in a handy position in his right boot. Throwing caution to the winds, he ran to the edge of the roof, hoping that the Count's feint would be sufficient cover; a full-scale firefight seemed to be raging down below, as the Count swept the slope with the twin machineguns. He certainly seemed to be making a devil of a din.

Otto took a deep breath and then, spitting on the palms of both hands in the manner of a labourer about to start on some really hard work, he grasped the rope, his heart beating wildly. Next instant he had swung himself out into space, feeling a great burning wrench in his shoulder muscles. For a moment he hung there, totally shocked by the sudden pain, hanging some twenty metres above the ground. Then he realized the danger of his position. If he didn't move soon, he'd fall off. *He had to start moving!*

Hand over hand he started to move forward, feet entwined in the rope, muscles ablaze with agony, his breath coming in harsh, gulping gasps. His hands were on fire now; his lungs sounding like cracked old leathern bellows. Still he climbed on desperately. Now he was nearly halfway there. He could see the opposite bunker quite clearly now. He forced himself to clamber on.

Suddenly the rope sagged alarmingly. Just in time he caught himself from falling. He was exactly in the centre of the rope and it was sagging under his weight.

'*Stoi!*' a challenge rang out in the darkness below.

Otto froze.

He had been spotted. He tensed there, waiting for the

hard steel to come ripping upwards into his soft, defence-less flesh.

But Otto was to live to fight another day.

Behind him in the bunker he had just left, the Count fired another flare. Immediately, the Russian who had challenged him dived for cover, anxious to get out of range of those vicious twin machine-guns, and commenced pumping shot after shot at bunker Number Four.

Otto almost dropped from his rope with sheer relief and started to clamber on, his whole body wracked with pain, sobbing with the strain, his eyes wide and wild with fear, his only thought being to reach the other bunker before he dropped off from exhaustion. At last he made it, and flopped down on the roof of bunker Number Five, oblivious to everything. For minutes he could only lie there in a wretched, sweat-soaked heap, gasping feverishly for air like a stranded fish.

He was in position at last.

ELEVEN

Otto's body tingled with expectancy as he crouched at the edge of the shaft. The two tommy-guns were lying on the turf next to him. He sensed fear-laced excitement, for he knew in a moment he would have to commence the last and most dangerous part of his mission.

He cocked his head to one side and listened, hearing the faint buzz of voices from below. It was impossible to make out how many of them were down there. The Count's guess was that it would take a dozen men or so to man a cannon of that calibre. Otto sniffed. Twelve to one. Hardly the kind of odds his mother, the Witch, would have gone for in the old days when she used to bet on the gee-gees at the Berlin Derby. Still, he had to accept them.

Back in bunker Number Four, he had considered trying to knock out the cannon by planting a grenade down its barrel, but the Count had advised against it. 'Besides, Otto,' he had added in warning, 'if the cannon happens to have just been fired when you want to work yourself along it, the barrel will be red-hot.'

Imagining all too vividly the damage the barrel could do to his most precious organ as he straddled it, working his way towards the muzzle, Otto had decided with a shudder against that particular method of attack.

Then he had toyed with the idea of simply tossing hand grenades down the air-shaft. Now he knew that method might fail too, for the angle at the bend could easily stop them. No, there was no other way. He had to clamber down the shaft himself and tackle the Popovs. He knew it was terribly dangerous. But he did have the advantage of surprise on his side and, with a bit of luck – *a helluva lot of luck, friend!* the cynical little voice at the back of his brain sneered – the smoke grenade might well do the trick.

'Adolf,' Otto said, raising his head to the night sky, 'the things I do for you, mate.' Then, grabbing one of the tommy-guns and pushing it in front of him, he entered the shaft face first, aware as he did so of a faint rapping noise coming from below which he couldn't quite identify.

'By the Black Virgin of Kazan!' Shukov cursed angrily, as the morse-key stopped clattering and the operator handed him the new message from the scouts. 'What kind of rabble are those partisans?' Angrily he dropped the message to the floor of the bunker.

'I didn't put it on the message-form, Comrade Captain,' the operator explained. 'But the scouts said it was a unit made up of women.'

Sergeant Kirov's comment was little different from that of Peiper's radio operator. 'What a waste!' he cried, and pressed the tip of his big thumb between two fingers the size of sausages. 'Fuck they should, not fight!'

The others laughed, but Shukov's face remained grim. 'Damn the Fritzes!' he snapped angrily. 'Operator, find out their exact position at this moment – grid reference, the lot.'

'*Da, da . . . Horoscho,*' the operator answered, and swung back to his key. Next instant he was rapping out the request for information.

'What's up, Comrade Captain?' Kirov asked. 'You said they were only little fish that we weren't going to bother about.'

Shukov nodded his agreement. 'Yes, I did. But listen to those trigger-happy kulaks out there.' He gestured to the infantry, still returning the Count's fire with wild abandon. 'Just imagine what those peasant shits would do if a Fritz armoured column suddenly loomed up out of nowhere tonight.'

'Don't draw me a picture, Comrade,' Kirov said easily. 'They'd tuck their big feet under their arms and run like hell.'

'Exactly.'

'So?'

'So, Kirov, we've got to stop the Fritzes before they get here. I hate to waste the ammo on such a trivial target, but I can't afford to have those infantrymen doing a bunk. If they do, we're left here without infantry protection, and—' Shukov hesitated, not wanting to frighten his men altogether, loyal and brave as they had all proved themselves '—I don't have to tell you what kind of weapons the Fritzes would use against this bunker, however ineffectual they might be.'

Even Sergeant Kirov paled at the thought. 'Flame-throwers?' he said, his voice suddenly hushed.

Shukov nodded.

The gunners looked at each other.

Hurriedly Shukov attempted to reassure them. 'Don't worry, this place is secure against everything but a direct hit by a ton-weight bomb, and I doubt if the Fritzes would ever be able to plant anything on us – even if they *had* a bomb that size, Comrades. Still we can't have those stubble-hoppers running—'

'Comrade Captain,' the operator's voice cut into Shukov's words. His morse-key had commenced clattering again moments before, and now, once more, he was bent over his pad, eyes narrowed in the poorly-lit bunker, taking down the information transmitted by the scouts who were shadowing Peiper's column.

Shukov swung round and peered over his shoulder as he started to scribble down the details.

'*Horoscho!*' he snapped, as the morse-key ceased chattering. 'All right, Comrades, they're less than ten kilometres away now, nicely bunched together. To work!'

Obediently the gunners commenced their task. Two of them swung open the great breech and started to thrust home the huge wads of propellant; two others pushed it further up the breech by means of a ramrod; while the ammunition numbers grunted and sweated, wrestling the enormous shells closer to the cannon. The layer swung himself behind his instruments, and as Captain Shukov rapped out his firing instructions, adjusted his dials and settings with expert skilled fingers. Then all was ready, and the gunners donned their flash-caps, replacing their helmets over the fire-proof white asbestos balaclavas, to wait in tense expectancy. All of them were silent now.

Dramatically, Captain Shukov strode up to the gun, taking care to keep to the right of the enormous breech, which came rearing back in metallic fury a good metre and a half when the gun was fired and would kill anyone standing behind it immediately with the tremendous impact. His eyes ran over the cannon. Everything was in order. He flashed a glance down to his watch and making a mental calculation of exactly where the Fritz column would be at this precise moment, began to count off the seconds.

Suddenly there was a soft clattering noise directly above his head. He looked up annoyed, his concentration ruined. 'What the damn was that?' he demanded angrily, looking up at the extractor shaft.

'Mice,' grunted Kirov, the chief loader, from his crouched position to the left of the breech; he was holding another great shell in his powerful arms, ready to ram it into the loading tray the instant the first one had been fired. 'These bunkers are lousy with them.'

'So,' Shukov snapped. 'All right then, we'll begin again.' This time he started to count off the ten seconds audibly, his voice somehow sounding very unnatural in the tense, threatening atmosphere.

'Nine . . . eight . . . seven . . . six . . .'

*

Peiper's vehicles were now advancing in a wild 'V' formation, speeding recklessly through the darkness, ignoring the tracer hurtling towards them from both sides like golden, glowing ping-pong balls. A shell exploded just above Peiper's lead half-track. He ducked instinctively, feeling the hot air of the explosion burn his back and hearing the hair at the small of his neck crackle as it was singed. Shrapnel hissed wildly through the air.

But Peiper was too exhilarated by the wildness of this crazy night attack to be afraid. Another bunch of surprised Russian infantry loomed up out of the glowing darkness. Instinctively he pressed the trigger of the deck machine-gun. The slugs ripped into them, galvanizing them into mad electric movement; the next instant they fell to the ground, dead and dying.

A burst of 20mm shells hissed through the air to the right. One of the half-tracks reared up in the air, like a horse being put to the saddle for the first time, then crashed down its left track flopping loose and powerless like a broken limb. The panzer grenadiers inside were uninjured. Expertly, they dropped over the sides of the crippled vehicle and doubled through the tracer to the next half-track.

'*That's the stuff, boys!*' Peiper yelled. '*At 'em like Blücher! Hit 'em with a sockful of shit!*'

They rolled on. Now, to their immediate front, as the Russian infantry panicked and commenced to break, alarm flares started to shoot into the night sky on all sides. Red, green and white, they sailed upwards, to burst into brilliant flame. For the first time, Peiper could see what was waiting for him on the formidable heights up ahead: a series of squat, low, powerful-looking forts, each one of them seemingly armed with a long overhanging cannon, the like of which he had never seen in all his career as a soldier. '*The Miropol Position!*' he breathed.

'Holy strawsack!' Heinze gasped, hanging on grimly next to him in the wildly shaking half-track as it raced across the steppe at fifty kilometres an hour. 'Clap your glassy orbs on that, Hauptsturm!'

Peiper's heart sank. To the immediate right of the bunker-line, one of the monsters, outlined an ominous blood-red in the light of a sudden flare, was beginning to raise itself into the air. He knew what that meant. The great cannon was about to open fire.

'Sevitvre . . . tri . . . dva . . .'

Otto's knowledge of Russian was exceedingly limited, but the sudden movement down below and the noise the cannon had made as it had been raised told him all he needed to know. The Popovs were about to fire. He could hesitate no longer. Groping awkwardly for the smoke grenade tucked into the side of his boot, he took a deep breath, prepared to propel himself from the tight confines of the shaft, and pulled out the pin.

'Odjin,' Shukov cried and prepared to bring down his hand in the signal for 'fire'.

But it was not to be. There was a clatter. Metal struck stone. Shukov looked down, startled. A small round object had rolled to a stop in the centre of the floor. 'What—'

'Grenade!' Kirov's cry of alarm cut into his question.

Next instant it exploded with a soft plop, and almost immediately, thick white smoke began to stream from it.

'Alarm . . . alarm!' Shukov cried, desperately tugging for his pistol, as the cloud of white rose up about his knees.

'Rukki verk!' a heavily accented voice cried in Russian.

Suddenly out of nowhere a strange figure had appeared, tommy-gun thrust forward menacingly. As if to emphasize his order, the stranger fired a swift burst. Chips of concrete erupted violently from the wall just behind Shukov's head and the chamber was suddenly filled with the deafening chatter of automatic fire.

Kirov dropped his shell and rushed at the lone civilian. He cried something in German which Shukov couldn't understand – perhaps it was a warning. Next instant he pressed the trigger of his tommy-gun. Kirov screamed shrilly and went down, arms fanning the air, as if he were trying to climb the rungs of an invisible ladder.

'*Rukki verk!*' the stranger ordered once again and swung the smoking tommy-gun from left to right.

The terrified gunners seemed to give up all thought of resistance. Their arms shot up frantically, like school-children begging to be excused.

Otto breathed an inward sigh of intense relief. He had pulled it off. Then he felt a sudden warm-damp sensation on his left leg, and knew that it wasn't blood. For him it was too late to be excused. He had pissed himself!

TWELVE

Dawn.

Otto studied his prisoners, who were squatting tamely in one corner of the bunker. All the fight seemed to have gone out of them and they were silent now, save for the wounded Kirov, who although tough enough to survive ten slugs in the guts instead of the one that had hit him and stopped his sudden rush, was groaning with pain at regular intervals. Still holding his tommy-gun in one hand, Otto peered through the central periscope.

Outside, the new sun was rising reluctantly, as if hesitant to illuminate the crazy landscape of death and destruction. Everywhere there were shattered trucks and half-tracks; the corpses left after the night's death hung on the rusty wire like abandoned bundles of rags, abandoned by the Russian infantry as they fled before Peiper's crazy thrust; further to the rear, Peiper's surviving vehicles and the new ones were streaming towards the bunker from the west, raising swirling clouds of dust.

Otto gave a smile of satisfaction. It was time to contact the big blond fools of the Bodyguard before they got it into their thick wooden skulls to make an attack on the bunker-line. He had waited for first light because he hadn't wanted to have his turnip shot off in the darkness. Now it was light enough for the men down below to see that it was him.

Suddenly Otto gasped and the smile rapidly vanished from his face. A small group of crouched figures in the green mottled camouflage of the Bodyguard had impinged on the gleaming glass of the periscope to the left. Stealthily, they were working their way around the littered and abandoned weapon pits towards the blind side of Bunker Number Five, two of them armed with a frighteningly familiar weapon. Otto gulped. It was that cake-arse Hairless Horst and his flame-throwers. They had to surrender, and surrender quick – either that or have their eggs fried off. He swung round and jerked up his tommy-gun threateningly. 'All right, you lot, we're going out. Come on, on yer feet, *davoi*!'

Hurriedly the Russians scrambled to their feet. Plainly they understood the gesture, if they didn't understand the words.

With another jerk of his tommy-gun, Otto indicated that a couple of the gunners should lift Kirov; this they did, with Otto looking on suspiciously.

'You,' he nodded to Captain Shukov, 'open the door.' With his free hand he made an opening gesture.

'*Da, da, ya, ponemyu*,' Shukov said hurriedly. 'Understand . . . understand.' He began to turn the catches which locked the steel door to the rear of the bunker, while Otto waited impatiently, already visualizing the horrifying results of those awesome weapons if they didn't get out before Hairless Horst got within range. At last the door swung open and the fresh morning air streamed into the smelly bunker. Obediently the gunners started to shuffle towards the exit.

'*Stop!*' Otto cried suddenly.

They came to a ragged halt and looked at him inquiringly.

'Don't give me any of those damn stupid looks!' Otto said in exasperation. 'You don't know that arse with ears, Hairless Harry. We need a white flag, or he'll toast the testicles off yer hair Popov arses!'

Shukov gaped at him. '*Sto?*' he queried.

'Don't you "*sto*" me! Something white! We need a flag of surrender!' Otto shot another wild look through the periscope. Hairless Harry's group had already vanished into the dead ground. Recalling the exercise he had viewed in what seemed now another age, Otto could just see them running all-out to get within firing range. The frightening thought lent urgency to his words. 'White!' he cried. '*Flag!*' he added desperately, hoping the word was the same in Russian, making a great show of waving a flag from side to side, a beatific smile of surrender on his face.

Shukov's eyes lit up. '*Flag*,' he repeated. Obviously the word was the same in Russian. '*Biely?*'

'Yes, *white!*' Frantically Otto searched his own pockets. His handkerchief had vanished. 'Vests, underpants, hand-kerchieves, *anything white!*' he cried. 'Come on! Tempo! Tempo! *Davoi!*'

'Underpants?' Shukov said stupidly, obviously wonder-ing if this young Fritz who had entered their lives so dramatically had gone off his head. 'Russki soldier nix underpants.' He puffed out his chest proudly. 'Underpants only officer. Nix soldier.'

Like a drowning man clutching at straws, Otto seized on this last chance. 'Get 'em off – at once!'

'Off – what?' Shukov gasped, wondering now to what strange fate he was going to be subjected.

Otto raised his tommy-gun threateningly and the others shrank back against the wall, hands raised in surrender. 'Get them knickers off at the double, Popov, or I won't guarantee for nothing!'

The threat worked. Hastily, while his former soldiers stared at him in wide-eyed amazement, Shukov started to pull off his boots and breeches to reveal a pair of ankle-length, off-white underpants, poorly patched at both knees with red flannel.

Shukov looked at Otto in fearful expectation.

'Off with 'em! Quick, for Chrissake, man! They're almost on to us. Quick!' He jerked up the muzzle of his automatic.

Rapidly Shukov pulled them off and stood there, knock-kneed and trembling all over, his shirt-tail pulled down firmly over his genitals. Hastily, Otto snatched the patched underpants from his hand and cried, 'At the double now! Outside – *davoi . . . davoi!*' In a confused rush the group streamed out, with Otto bringing up the rear, waving the underpants above his head for all he was worth, crying at the little group of men poised only fifty metres away. 'Don't shoot – don't shoot, Comrades! We're surrendering. Honest. It's me – Otto! *Don't shoot!*'

Sergeant Major Hartung, who had been carefully concealing himself behind the leading flame-thrower operator (for he wasn't the bravest of men) straightened up in an instant, as if someone had just planted a boot up his ample bottom. 'Christ on a crutch,' he bellowed, 'it's true! It's that smart-arsed civvie Stahl!'

Behind him, a bespectacled photographer from *Das Schwarze Korps*[1], an even more devout coward than the Sergeant Major, raised his Leica. He had a shrewd notion that the recording of this historic moment, would ensure that he'd be flown straight back to Berlin and far away from this nasty business in Russia, where people – even photographers – were liable to get killed.

Luck was on his side: the participants arranged themselves into a dramatic tableau which made the picture one of the classics of German wartime photography, ranking with that of the Führer entering the burning ruins of Warsaw in '39 and the Wehrmacht marching past the *Arc de Triomphe* one year later. The 'Surrender of the Miropol Position', as it has been called ever since, is never missing from any illustrated account of the war in Russia. To one side are the flame-thrower group, tense and crouched, as if about to go into action; to the other, a straggle of Russian prisoners, led by an officer, who for some reason was minus his trousers. In the centre stands a smiling, if ragged young civilian armed with a tommy-gun and waving some sort of improvised white flag, advancing on a giant NCO,

[1] publication of the Armed SS.

whose ruddy face bore a look of complete and utter amazement . . .

'Doctor Livingstone, I presume?' Hitler commented when he saw the picture; then, when he realized that his staff had not understood, he added, airing the encyclopaedic knowledge for which he was justly famous, 'The American Stanley greeting the long-lost Englishman Dr Livingstone in the middle of the African jungle in the nineteenth century.' Then he peered more closely at the photograph through his nickel spectacles and said to Himmler who had proudly brought him the photograph of the great event: 'I say, Heinrich, what's that bolshevik doing without his trousers, eh?'

But for that overwhelming question, Heinrich Himmler, the sallow-faced head of the SS, had no answer.

BOOK THREE: AFRICA

'*Mitgegangen, mitgefangen, mitgehangen*'.[1]

Old German Saying

[1] gone with, caught with, hanged with.

ONE

Outside it was snowing again. Great soft, wet, melancholy flakes floating down as if they had all the time in the world.

For two weeks now the weather in Southern Russia had been deteriorating rapidly. Every day since the beginning of November it had snowed. But the snow hadn't remained for long. In the afternoons it had melted, turning the ground into a sea of black mud into which the vehicles sank up to their axles, to be pulled free by gallant little *panje* horses, sweating and straining, their mud-stained flanks wet with sweat.

At night it was unearthly cold, and a bitter wind raced in straight from Siberia, freezing the sentries' breath and causing icicles to form on their nostrils and eyelashes. Even thinking became a major effort in the icy conditions. To try to fight off the fiendish cold, the soldiers wrapped themselves in layer after layer of clothing, all of it ridden with lice, and wrapped their hands in rags. But since that made their fingers too clumsy for them to fire their weapons, they attached twigs and little bits of wood to the awkward bundles of their fists and fired the machine-guns by wedging them into the triggers.

Food was a never-ending problem, too. What little butter the soldiers received with their rations had to be broken apart with an ice-axe and sucked in small pieces as 'butter-ice'. Bread had to be sawn into slices, then thawed out over a fire. The result was diarrhoea. All the soldiers suffered from it.

Frostbite was rampant too, especially in the feet. The Germans hadn't yet cottoned on to the Russian soldier's trick of taking a pair of boots one size too large and packing the extra space with straw or newspapers to keep out the cold. The German Army standard boots, 'dice-breakers' as the soldiers called them, were all equipped with steel nails, which were an ideal conductor for the cold, so that by the time a soldier had done half an hour's guard duty outside, his feet were frozen solid.

But the frost attacked not only the troopers' feet; it hit their weapons too. The oil froze in their machine-guns and rifles, preventing them from firing. Tanks wouldn't start. There was no special grease for the sights of the bigger cannon, so that the glass was permanently steamed over and the gunners couldn't fire.

All was greyness and bitter cold.

Otto, oblivious to the chatter of the Bodyguard's officers all around him, stared miserably out of the window of the commissar's villa. Even to his untrained eye, it was clear that the Wehrmacht generals had failed, through not being prepared for the Russian winter. The steam had gone out of the great offensive. The 'great anti-Bolshevik crusade', as the Gift-Dwarf's[1] newspapers were still calling it, had come to nothing; now it was going to be a bitter, hard slog. Despite the comfort of the roaring tiled stove in the corner, Otto, muffled up in a woman's fur-coat and felt ear-flaps, wished he was far away from here. He had had enough of the 'workers' paradise' and everything that went with it.

He watched as a group of young SS men slogged by, bent under the weight of great steaming soup kettles, which they were obviously taking out to the front-line positions. They didn't look good. Their faces were pale, strained and unshaven, and their skinny shoulders were bent as they trudged through the drifting snow, eyes fixed unseeingly on the ground, as if they bore all the cares of the world. Otto frowned. Could Dietrich really capture Rostov, his objective in the new winter offensive which

---

[1] Nickname for the German Minister of Propaganda, Dr Goebbels.

was about to commence in forty-eight hours' time? In these conditions? Somehow he doubted it.

'Penny for them, Otto,' a familiar voice chimed in, interrupting his reverie.

Otto turned slowly. It was the Count, heavily clad in an ankle-length greatcoat with a fur collar, his feet looking enormous and slightly ridiculous in a pair of felt-lined Russian *valenki* boots which he had bought on the black market. As usual he was wearing his monocle; he had begun to affect it as soon as they had been publicly hailed as the 'Heroes of Miropol', claiming that it gave him the 'necessary senior officer's look'.

'Not worth it, Count,' he answered gloomily. Morosely, he turned to stare at the officers, all of them wearing their new decorations, who were beginning to group themselves around the festive table.

'Why so sad, Otto?' the Count asked. 'We're warm here and there's a really splendid meal laid on for us. Haupsturmbannführer Peiper shot a roebuck while on reconnaissance yesterday, so there'll be venison.' He smiled winningly at his sour-faced companion. 'And a little birdie whispered in my ear that the mess officer has – er – organized some real caviare and pink Crimean champers. Things could be worse, much worse.'

'Could they?' Otto asked, nodding to the ration party trudging miserably through the snow. 'Do you know what those poor shits at the front will be getting their biters into this midday? Giddiup goulash and dead man's toes[1], and if they're very lucky indeed, a roof-hare[2].'

The Count's smile vanished; he was a kind man, who hated to see others suffer. 'I know, I know, Otto. It's very hard on the soldiers. Sometimes I don't know how those brave boys up there in the line stand it under these terrible conditions.'

'If I had my way—'

[1] Horsemeat goulash and hard-tack biscuits.
[2] A cat.

'*Meine Herren*,' Panzermeyer's hard voice cut into Otto's words. 'The General!'

The officers clicked to attention as General Dietrich entered, followed by Lehmann, both sporting their new decorations and both obviously in high good humour. Dietrich waved his hand for them to stand at ease.

'Gentlemen, let us regard this as the condemned man's last meal. Only forty-eight more hours and we're off again – and this time let's fillet Stalin's guts for good.' With that he nodded to a white-coated SS orderly, who pulled back the chair at the head of the table smartly so that Dietrich could be seated. 'Let us make the most of it, gentlemen.' He extended his hand winningly to Otto and the Count – the guests of honour – to sit on both sides of him, and there was a buzz of chatter and the scraping of chairs as the officers began to sit down.

Dietrich started the meal ceremonially enough. As soon as the mess waiters had filled their glasses with the sparkling Crimean champagne, he rose and raised his glass, beaming to left and right. 'Gentlemen, I give you a toast to those two men who helped most of you present to cure your throatache this summer.'

There was a ripple of laughter, and here and there an officer touched his newly-awarded Knight's Cross.

'To Herr Stahl – *nomen es omen*' – as Dietrich aired his sole Latin tag, Otto groaned inwardly. How often had he heard that phrase, and how often had it signalled trouble and danger for him – 'and Graf von der Weide. *To the Conquerors of Miropol!*'

'*To the Conquerors of Miropol!*' the others chorused. The Count beamed back at them, red-faced with pride and happiness, but as Otto stared down at the looted damask tablecloth, his handsome face looked decidedly unhappy.

Dietrich sat down again and gestured to the mess waiter to place a bottle of champagne directly in front of him, so that he could help himself as often as he wished. 'Gentlemen,' he said, as the waiters started to distribute the caviare heaped on squares of pumpernickel and decorated with slices of lemon, 'this day, I'm really going to buy one. That Jew von Manstein's plan for Rostov has got more holes in it than the whores in a Munich knocking-shop. Careful tonsils, because I'm going to try to drown you this day!'

Laughing happily, Dietrich and his officers turned to the serious business of drinking.

At the door to the kitchen, the Russian serving-maid Tasya, dressed in a too-tight black dress that revealed her ample charms in all their glory, her face red and plump beneath her frilled serving cap, nodded to Glinka, the cook, who was basting the roebuck under the watchful eye of Sergeant Major Hartung. On account of the kitchen's warmth and the potential it offered for amorous conquests, Hairless Horst had made it his unofficial HQ ever since the offensive had come to an end.

As planned, Tasya bent down low, as if she were doing up the buckle of her black patent-leather shoes, revealing a length of sturdy black-stockinged leg with above a fair portion of milky white flesh. Hartung swallowed hard, as if he had suddenly choked on a bone. His big face went crimson and his pig-like little eyes narrowed. With a hand that trembled slightly, he smoothed back his non-existent hair and said thickly: '*Grr*, I'd like to get my flippers on that! I'd eat it with a silver spoon, I would!'

Preoccupied as he was, the excited Sergeant Major failed to notice Glinka taking his ladle and striking it against the dull red glowing stove-pipe. It was the signal.

'It's on, Comrades!' Olga said hastily, as the hollow clang rang out in the freezingly cold cellar. '*Horoscho!* Start playing out the wires.'

The six women soldiers of the Partisan Battalion needed no urging; they all knew that they were in grave danger every minute they stayed in the Fascist camp. They had smuggled themselves into the Bodyguard's camp dressed as peasant women, selling the tiny dried fish of the area to the hungry soldiers, who fortunately for them, were prepared to eat anything these days and prized the bone-dry, smelly, sardine-like fish as a delicacy. Little did the eager soldiers know that under the fish, lay stick after stick of gelignite.

Covered by Olga's drawn pistol, the women played out the wires leading from the explosive, which was positioned directly beneath the commissar's dining-room, threading them into the hole which they had made in the cellar wall. Outside, another of the 'peasant women' drew the wires into Dietrich's personal thunderbox, which Olga had reasoned – correctly, as it turned out – no one would dare use. If they had, they would have been in for a great surprise, for at this very moment, squatting on its well-scrubbed seat next to the neatly-cut squares of newspaper (for General Dietrich was a stickler for 'correctness', as he called it – even in his thunderbox), was yet another peasant woman, clasping a detonator box to her ample bosom.

Finally they were finished, and Olga gave the lines of wire a hasty check. They were in order. They fitted exactly into the sticks of explosive. Nothing could go wrong now. '*Horoscho!*' she hissed. 'All is well, Comrades. Leave at one-minute intervals by the back door. Annya, you first!'

One by one, the hefty peasants tip-toed up the stairs that led to the kitchen and past Hairless Horst, whose thoughts were far too much taken up with the mountains of warm, white, female flesh that lay beneath Tasya's too-tight dress to notice their departure. Finally it was Olga's turn. Now that the others had gone and could not see her weakness, tears sprang to her eyes – for she had seen her betrayer Otto, whom she still loved, enter the doomed villa only one hour before. She gazed up at the roof. Up there sat the man who had scorned her love, enjoying his last meal on this earth. '*Dostvedanya*, little Otto,' she whispered huskily, hiding her pistol beneath her peasant's apron.

'And I *did* love you so.' Then she wiped away her tears. Now she must be hard. Clicking to attention, she raised her massive fist in the Communist salute. 'Comrade Stalin,' she said to the blank wall in a serious formal voice, 'I beg to report the death of the entire staff of the Adolf Hitler Bodyguard Division!' Then she was gone.

'*Meine Herren,*' Dietrich announced, his speech slightly slurred. As he rose to his feet, he dropped his second 'dead soldier' to the floor, where it joined a heap of other empty champagne bottles. 'The *pièce de résistance!*' He gestured to the door, where a red-faced, straining Hairless Horst, assisted by two mess waiters, had appeared bearing an enormous mound of vari-coloured ice, formed into the shape of a bunker, with a long gun made of red ice sticking out of it.

Otto's mouth dropped open stupidly. Even before Dietrich explained what it was, he recognized it. 'Oh, my aching arse, Count,' he gasped, 'it's the Miropol Position – done in ice-cream!'

Spontaneously, the red-faced, drunken officers broke into excited applause, as Hairless Horst, followed by the anxious waiters, staggered to the table, to deposit the back-breaking dessert with a sigh of relief in its centre.

Dietrich beamed at the Count and drew his ceremonial dagger, bearing the old SS legend '*My honour is loyalty*'. With a grand gesture he offered it to the Count. 'Here, my dear Graf. Let me give you the honour of carving the first portion.'

The Count rose to his feet, blushing with pride. 'Words fail me, my dear General. Who would have thought . . .'

He stopped suddenly. For some inexplicable reason, the great mass of ice had begun to tremble. Not only that, but small pieces of plaster had begun to rain down from the ceiling. The Count flashed a wild, puzzled look at the General, dagger poised absurdly in mid-air, and then another one back at the ice-cake, which was now definitely beginning to tilt to one side, observed by the officers in petrified awe.

Now not only the cake was trembling, but the whole house. Smoke was beginning to pour from cracks which had suddenly opened up in the wall. The door of the green-tiled oven flew open and a mass of red-hot embers poured out on to the floor.

And then the charges exploded in full force. It was as if some monstrous hand had smacked into the walls of the villa. There was a terrifying cracking noise. Bricks hurtled down. Glass smashed. Timbers came roaring down. The whole house seemed to be squeaking and groaning, dust spurting from the cracks opening up on all sides, filling the air with the dryness of centuries.

Panic erupted. Suddenly completely sober, the officers tried to run for cover as the floors tilted upwards, forcing them to labour up them as if they were climbing a steep mountain slope.

Otto collided with Dietrich as they both tried to avoid the avalanche of ice-cake which was heading straight for them. The Count was not so quick. He disappeared beneath a mound of ice-cream, spluttering and gasping with the shock, the impact knocking him on his back, his legs waving furiously, his upper body completely swamped. With all his strength, Otto grabbed him and pulled him to his feet, spitting out ice and trying to clear it from his eyes. 'Come on!' he gasped above the ever-increasing roar. 'Outside, Count . . . *For Chrissake, move it!*'

Somehow, as the house began to collapse around them, blazing timbers tumbling from the gables and trapping screaming officers everywhere, or felling them with skull-crushing impact – somehow, the two friends staggered out through the black, choking smoke into the garden. But even here, flurries of stone and flying slate were ripping into the firs and through the snowy air in a tremendous hushing, sucking blast. Suddenly Otto felt a stinging blow in his right shoulder and staggered in mid-stride, a tremendous wave of unbearable agony welling up in his body. He wanted to drop, the shock was so great. But he knew that would be the end. He *had* to get as far away from the villa as possible. Staggering on, his blood dripping onto the snow behind him, he willed himself forward.

Bent as if against a powerful gale, the blast whipping their clothes tightly against their bodies, the two of them struggled on, clambering over the shrapnel-riddled corpse of a mess waiter collapsed grotesquely on a trayful of glasses. The Count's monocle shattered. Half-blinded by the sudden spider's web of glass, he tumbled from side to side, supporting the bleeding Otto as best he could, heading for the shelter of an outhouse, where the pig carcasses, the division's meat supply for the week, trembled violently on their hooks, as if miraculously restored to life. Behind them the villa was burning furiously now. Officers, their uniforms ablaze, staggered out, screaming furiously before collapsing in the snow, writhing back and forth in their death agony.

'Come on, Otto,' the Count choked. 'Only a few more metres! Keep going, old friend!'

Before Otto's eyes, scarlet and silver shells seemed to be exploding. His eyes started to roll upwards. His legs felt as if they were made of rubber. He couldn't feel the ground any more. 'Count . . .' he stuttered, trembling like a frightened animal, 'let me go . . . Save yourself . . .'

'No!' the Count snapped firmly. 'Keep going. I *order* you to keep going! Only a few more metres . . .'

Otto had a rush of vague, half-conscious impressions: of two men covered in thick dust, clinging to each other in terror like lovers carved in stone in a public park; an open-mouthed, bewildered man standing naked in a zinc-bath filled with water; the engine of a guard-tank on fire, its tracer ammunition exploding and zig-zagging upwards in crazy profusion, like some lethal firework display; the branches of a fir-tree strangely and inexplicably filled with hanging human limbs; a head rolling across their path, the lips set in a toothy smile – and all the time, above it all, the Count's voice, a million kilometres away now, urging him to keep on staggering forward.

Then it happened.

The shed containing the dancing pig carcasses suddenly blew apart. A great half-side of pig came hurtling straight towards them. The Count stopped instinctively, propping Otto up as best he could. It was as if he knew that their fate had been decided; that there was no escaping what was about to happen.

Next instant the carcass slammed into them. They dropped as if pole-axed. The carcass flew on straight in the greedy maws of that purple flame, where it would be duly roasted to a cinder, much to the chagrin of the starved rescuers later.

Finally the massacre was over, and Otto and the Count lay still, sprawled out in the bloody carnage of that body-littered garden, while the snowflakes drifted down and began to cover the corpses . . .

TWO

In the big barn, its floor covered with blood-stained straw, the wounded lay in long rows. Some were able to talk, some lying in dazed silence, others gasping harshly as if in their death-throes; some lay completely silent, either drugged or dead. Over all hung the heavy, cloying stench of spirit-disinfectant.

Otto rested his wounded shoulder against the damp wall, feeling it throb a little painfully, while next to him the Count examined his blue-and-green swollen face by means of a little hand mirror, making little tut-tut noises every so often, obviously not at all pleased with the damage the flying pig carcass had inflicted on his fleshily handsome face.

Otto grinned in spite of the pain. The Count was a vain old shit, but he had to admit the old boy's mug certainly did look a sight. Then he turned his attention to Doctor Hackebeil, the Bodyguard's chief surgeon, who had now entered the tent, followed by a small group of assistant doctors and a handful of medical orderlies. As usual, he was carrying the surgical chopper for which he was famous throughout the Division. As he was often given to declaring, 'Chopper's the name and chopper's my instrument.'[1]

Now he moved from man to man, making a quick examination of their wounds and then rapping out a swift order, waving the gleaming instrument to emphasize his words. Here and there a man was ordered out of the barn and carried away hurriedly by the orderlies, groaning miserably; obviously, he knew what his fate was going to

[1] *Hackebeil* is roughly 'chopper' in German.

be. Others had strange red discs placed on their foreheads by the orderlies. But for the most part, Hackebeil contented himself with scribbling a few indecipherable words on the man's wound-card.

In due course he came to Otto's place on the floor. Bending over low, so that Otto could smell the vodka on his breath – it was rumoured that Hackebeil consumed a litre of the stuff before breakfast – he examined the young man's bandaged shoulder. He brought his big, pitted, scarlet drinker's nose closer to the wound and sniffed hard. 'Beautiful, Mr Hero of Miropol,' he declared, satisfied. 'Not a whiff of gangrene! You'll have a nice old scab-and-matter pie back there soon, but you'll keep your arm, Hero.' So saying, he beamed at Otto, swung his cleaver and passed on to the Count.

'Good God!' he exclaimed, seeing the Count's puffed-up, mottled face for the first time, from which two tiny eyes peered out from swollen slits. 'What hit you, my dear Count – a kitchen sink?'

'No,' the Count answered miserably, 'a flying pig.'

There was a ripple of laughter from the assistant doctors. Hackebeil grinned too, and pulling out a silver flask, took a hefty slug of vodka. He gasped, belched and replaced the flask, his red eyes suddenly wet and glowing. 'Antiseptic, you know,' he said, to no one in particular. 'Keeps out the germs.' Gently he prodded the Count's swollen cheeks and then ordered him to open his mouth.

If the Count could have blushed, he would undoubtedly have done so; for while he was unconscious, someone had removed his precious false teeth. Now they could be found nowhere and vain as he was, the Count hardly dared open his mouth, even to speak. Hesitantly he did as he was ordered.

For a few moments Doctor Hackebeil poked around in the Count's mouth with his gloved hand, for it was freezing in the barn. 'Blast blew out yer biters, I see, but otherwise no damage there.'

After bending down to scribble something on the label attached to the Count's blanket, he passed on to Hairless Horst, who lay in a drugged sleep, making a harsh snoring noise. To Otto's surprise, Hackebeil didn't even bother to examine him. Presumably he could tell all he needed to know from Hairless Horst's ashen, shrunken face, the big nose now pinched and white.

'Red disc,' he ordered, and continued his rounds.

Otto beckoned to the bespectacled orderly at the end of the little group which trailed after Hackebeil. He knew the man slightly from before. He, too, came from Berlin-Wedding, and a couple of times they had exchanged memories of their place of birth. 'Hey, *Kumpel*,' he whispered, 'what gives with those red discs?'

The bespectacled Berliner looked up sharply, checking whether any of the doctors could overhear him, then bent down and whispered, 'It's the old bone-mender's system. In these forward dressing stations, he always divides the wounded into three groups – for simplicity's sake. There's one lot heading for the meat house—'

'Meat house?' Otto echoed, puzzled.

'Yeah, those we carry out. They're gonna snuff it and he doesn't want the rest of you to see 'em croak. Then there's the red discs like old Hairless Horst there, who's been hit in the eggs and needs really skilled treatment. They're for immediate evacuation for Germany. They're gonna take 'em out by air this afternoon, weather permitting.'

'And the rest?' Otto asked cautiously. 'Us lot?'

The Berliner grinned at him. 'Otto, you lucky lot are gonna live to fight another day.' He dug a finger in his skinny chest. 'We're gonna nurse you lot back to health, so that General Dietrich has enough cannon-fodder to win himself another putty medal.'

And with that, he passed on, leaving Otto to ponder the injustice of this life.

★

'Count,' Otto said hesitantly. Doctor Hackebeil and his entourage had departed, leaving the barn to the care of the orderlies, who were now passing from man to man, armed with chipped enamel bed-pans which they shoved roughly under the wounded, crying, 'Three minutes – piss, shit, or both! But you've only got three minutes. Now get on with it!'

'Yes, Otto,' the Count whispered, tight-lipped so as to hide his gaping gums, 'what is it?'

'I'd like to ask you a question. Haven't you had enough of Russia?'

'I must admit, Otto, that I'm not particularly pleased with it just at the moment. What a treacherous thing to do – blow us up like that, when we came to liberate them from the Bolshevik terror!' He took another look at his swollen face in the mirror. 'No – I'm not pleased with it at all!'

Otto sighed and flashed a look heavenwards, as if praying to God to give him patience with such fools. 'I think we ought to be evacuated.'

'But we've only got minor wounds – not like poor old Sergeant Major Hartung there.' He gestured to Hartung, who was still snoring harshly in a drugged sleep.

Otto sniffed. 'Well, I hardly think his poor little Gerda will miss it. *When I've had 'em, they stay had* – pooh!' He repeated Hairless Horst's boastful words with a disdainful snort. 'Listen – all we need is the red disc.'

The Count looked alarmed. 'Otto! Surely you wouldn't stoop so low as to steal them from these poor chaps?'

'Of course not, you silly shit! But there are other ways of getting them.'

'How do you mean?'

'What you've got beneath your head at this moment would do the trick nicely.'

The Count touched the pack which he was using as a pillow; it contained his personal effects, shaving kit and change of underwear.

'Yes, I know – you've been saving your ration of lung-torpedoes for the last month or so. You must have at least a thousand of them in there.'

'But Christmas is coming, Otto,' the Count protested. 'I was saving my cigarettes to buy certain things on the black market for my people back in the Reich.'

'Forget it,' Otto said airily. 'Those cancer-sticks are better than ten years' life insurance. They're going to get us the red discs – and back to mother.'

'How?'

'Just watch when those piss-pot merchants get up here. Now haul arse and give me two packets of twenty – quick!' In spite of the pain in his shoulder, Otto started to hum a dirty ditty happily to himself. They were going home! *They were going home!*

'*Tenente Marco Mortello*, at your service!'

Those who were still conscious – for the drive to the military airfield had taken five hours through a howling snowstorm – peered at the figure standing at the door of the freezing hangar.

Otto frowned. The officer standing there was surprisingly handsome, with a show of brilliant white teeth under a pencil-slim moustache, the hair peeping out from beneath his rakishly tilted cap gleaming with pomade and arranged in careful, tight waves. But somehow he couldn't make out the man's uniform. It was much more elegant than that of the Luftwaffe, and although he wore pilot's wings on his breast, he seemed to be carrying a small dagger at his trim corseted waist.

The harassed, overworked Luftwaffe doctor who was doing his best to cope with the flood of seriously wounded SS men, went over to the pilot in the strange uniform. 'You are to evacuate them?' he asked hastily.

'*Si, si,*' the officer replied, gloved hand still raised in salute. As his dark eyes swept across the badly wounded men lying in the blood-stained straw, they seemed to suddenly fill with sympathy. 'Ah, the poor ones, the poor ones!' Then, suddenly, he clapped his hands, crying '*Avanti, avanti . . . giovani Italiane!* The sons of the wolf fight side by side with their German comrades, while our women-folk succour their wounded—' breaking off abruptly as a flock of handsome young women, bosoms heaving and dark eyes flashing, burst into the room excitedly, their plump faces flushed with good health, and immediately started passing fruit among the soldiers, bending low to offer them drinks from wicker-covered bottles of chianti, careless of how much naked thigh they revealed as they did so.

'*Italians!*' the Count breathed. 'They're Italians!'

'Spaghetti-eaters!' Otto echoed, and opened his mouth expectantly as a beautiful young woman bent low as if tendering him one of her magnificent breasts, but in fact offering him a bunch of grapes.

Tenente Mortello watched happily for a few moments and then, turning to the dumbfounded Luftwaffe doctor, explained: 'In Rome, they have heard of the dastardly attack on the HQ of the Bodyguard. The Duce himself was informed and immediately ordered the Royal Italian Air Force to prepare to evacuate the brave wounded men of that same formation which has guarded his life so often in the past.'

Hardly able to believe his ears, Otto took his head out from between the two great breasts which were threatening to suffocate him – delightful as that particular fate might have been – and gasped excitedly, 'Did you hear that, Count? We've won the flower vase! Italy and Macaroni gash.' Delightedly he patted the Italian woman on her plump rump, which threatened to burst the tight black silk of her uniform skirt at any moment. 'At last I can take my salami out of mothballs!'

'*Si, si – salami!*' the beautiful Italian said eagerly. '*Vino, tutto!*'

'*And gasho!*' Otto cried uproariously, beside himself with joy at this wonderful change in his fortune. '*Molto gasho!*'

At the door, Tenente Mortello turned to observe the scene: the soldiers were now chewing contentedly on the fruit, taking great slugs of the red wine, and even the most seriously wounded of them were trying to get their hands up the Italian girls' skirts and pinching those ample bottoms. Beaming, he appealed for silence.

'Brave German comrades,' he announced grandly. 'For you the horror is over. The Duce has ordered that you will be accommodated at the best of our hospitals. There will be the best doctors, the best nurses.' He flung out his right arm from his elegant chest in a theatrical gesture. 'The best of everything!' He clicked to attention and flung them the fascist salute. 'In four hours, comrades, you will be in our fascist capital. *Roma!*'

'*Roma!*' Otto breathed and sank back on the straw, his mouth full of half-eaten grapes, his nostrils full of the glorious smell of woman. He had done it. He was shut of the workers' and peasants' paradise at last!

But four hours later, the two-engined wooden Savoia still hadn't reached *Roma*.

'It is a little strange,' Mortello said over the intercom, first in Italian for the benefit of the nurses, and then in German, 'but the map seems to have changed a bit. The Aegean Sea appears to be in the wrong place.'

Otto looked at the Count, but he didn't seem to be in the least bit worried. He was far too busy practising his Italian with one of the plump nurses. As always he forgot everything in the excitement of what he called a 'new adventure'.

'But never fear, brave German comrades and loyal fascist nurses! We will arrive in our glorious capital soon.'

Midnight came and still they hadn't reached Rome. Fuel

was running out and the co-pilot, Sergeant Massimi, a typically pessimistic Sicilian, was beginning to strap on his parachute in a very determined manner, as if it wouldn't be long now before he had to use it.

The pilot frowned and spoke into the intercom. 'A slight miscalculation, ladies and gentlemen, that's all. I see light below. I shall put down there.' Mortello strained his eyes. Down below he seemed to see the white of breakers and his face brightened. 'I have just spotted the Adriatic. All is well after all. We shall land on the shore.'

Otto swallowed hard as the plane began to dive, trying to ignore the little spluttering noises it made as the fuel started to run out. While he fought hard not to be sick, the Italian nurses next to him gave shrill little screams of fear and one of them knelt and crossed herself, praying fervently to the Virgin Mary. Otto's hopes of ever seeing *Roma* started to recede rapidly.

But however bad a navigator Mortello was, he proved to be an excellent pilot. Five minutes later he was braking the two-engined transport to a stop on a stretch of white sand, with the breakers striking the shore in a white flurry of excited water only fifty metres away.

'*Preggo!*' he announced proudly and slumped back in his seat happily. 'We are here . . . *Bella Italia!*'

But Lieutenant Mortello was wrong; this was not *Bella Italia*. Hardly had he opened the door of the Savoia than a group of coal-black soldiers appeared out of nowhere, all smoking pungent cigarettes, their long old-fashioned rifles slung carelessly over their backs as they trudged wearily across the sand.

'Soldiers to me!' Mortello called excitedly in Italian. 'Son of the Wolf rally here!'

Raggedly the soldiers came to a halt and stared at the elegant officer outlined in the green light of the instruments as he stood there in the door of the cockpit. Complete bewilderment was written all over their black broad faces.

Mortello repeated his order, but again there was no

response. He frowned angrily, and said, for the benefit of the wounded Germans, who were staring out curiously at the negroes, 'Presumably native troops from the Rome garrison. Their Italian will not be very good, I should—'

He broke off. A white man had pushed his way through the natives, a white *képi* tilted at a rakish angle on his shaven head and a white silk scarf thrown dramatically over his right shoulder. He halted and touched a gloved hand to his *képi*. '*Capitaine Lemercier, Régiment de Tirailleurs Sénégalais.*'

Mortello acknowledged the salute with a look of complete bewilderment. 'But why are you speaking French with me, *Capitano*?'

Lemercier frowned severely. 'Because I am French, *sale con!*'

'*Impossible!*'

'*Pas impossible!*' the French officer rapped back in irritation.

'But where – where *are* we?' Mortello stuttered. 'Not France . . . I couldn't have gone *that* far off course!'

'No, not France,' the Frenchman agreed.

Mortello attempted a smile at the thought that his navigation had been not so bad, but it vanished the very next instant.

'No, not France,' the Frenchman said grimly. 'But in *Afrique du Nord!*'

'*Afrique du Nord!*' Mortello exploded.

'*Mais oui.* To be exact – Algiers . . .'

THREE

'*Gash galore, gorgeous grub and no goddam war!*' That was
how, years later, Otto was wont to describe those months
in Algiers in the middle of World War Two. 'It was the
most beautiful time of my whole life. You'd never believe
how we all lived that year – the SS men, me and the Count,
Irma (that was my girl – well, most of the time she was),
the Macaroni officer and his sergeant, and those luscious
Eyetie nurses. What do the Amis call it? Yes, that's it – *a
shitting life of Riley!*'

The French officers hadn't been particularly pleased to
see the sudden appearance of a planeload of wounded men
from Hitler's premier SS Division; but in 1942, the Vichy
French were leaning over backwards not to offend their
German 'co-workers', and so, with the help of the officers
of the German Armistice Board, Otto soon arranged for
them all to be housed in a temporary hospital. It was a
beautiful white stucco villa set above the town not far from
the St George Hotel, one day to be Ike's HQ. Here they
would recover fully before being sent back to the Reich
and the war in Russia. Under pressure from the German
Armistice Commission, the French were even forced to
provide two doctors for the SS wounded, but with a
malicious sense of humour, they sent Docteur Valmy, a
hunch-backed VD specialist, and Docteur Solomon Hurwitz, a dark-skinned, hook-nosed gynaecologist. In the
end both their skills came in very useful for '*les sales cons
de la SS*' – as the French called them angrily behind their
backs – and their over-enthusiastic Italian nurses. But the
French weren't to know that.

'Of course,' Otto recalled much later, 'once the Count got his new plastic choppers made for him by some Frog down in the city, he was a dead loss as per usual. If he'd had his shitting way, we'd have been back at the Russian front toot-sweet having the eggs shot off us by the Popovs. But Mrs Stahl's handsome son wasn't having any of that lark. Not likely! I got 'em all organized. The Macaroni officer Mortello wasn't too keen to go back to *Bella Italia* as he always called it, cos' *Bella Italia* wasn't so shitting *bella* that year. I reckon he thought his days in the Royal Italian Air Force were numbered after that balls-up on the beach. He knew it was Russia for him. So he didn't exactly object when I appointed him Doctor Mortello, Chief Surgeon of the 1st SS Emergency Hospital. Whenever those fancy-pants of the Armistice Commission started to nose around the hospital, he always made a good front-man. Besides, he'd got pally with the frog officer Capitaine Lemercier. Turned out they had an interest in common – those lovely Arab lads who hung around the Kasbah in those days, flashing their eyes and wiggling their hips. Lovely creamcake-arses they had – if you like that sort of thing!'

In Algiers, that winter of 1942–43 passed swiftly as Otto, his shoulder now healed, went about his duties as Chief Supply Officer in the city, amply provided with francs from the Armistice Commission. He enjoyed getting the feel of the place. 'It looked like a shitting Austrian comic opera that winter. God, the uniforms alone! There were the Spahis in red cloaks, mounted on pure white nags, looking at yer as if to say, "one word from you, mate, and you'll be lacking a set of lugs." Those nobbly-kneed little buggers of the Chantiers de la Jeunesse – they were the Vichy youth movement, modelled on the Hitler Youth – dressed in green. Then there were those great swaggering toughs of the Foreign Legion, in their baggy white pants and *képis*, with a big old blue cummerbund wrapped round their waists. I always gave those hard-nosed buggers a wide berth.'

For hours on end Otto would saunter through the city, stopping at the sidewalk cafes to sip sticky, syrupy apéritifs with the refugees from France and the Arabs who sat for hours over their mint tea, waiting and watching, waiting and watching, Otto knew not for what. (It was only much later, when the Algerian War broke out, that he found the answer to that puzzling question.) At other times he would edge his way into the crowded bar of the Hotel Aletti mingling with the gorgeous French whores and the officers of the garrison who frequented the place; he ignored the Vichy slogan above the bar, '*Travail, Patrie, Famille*' – like all the rest, he had other things in mind at that moment.

Meanwhile Irma, a plump raven-eyed Italian nurse with breasts like melons gave him all he needed in bed – and more. 'Shit, some mornings I thought after a session with her that I hadn't any spine left. But it was lovely grub and I couldn't get enough of it. After all, I'd had my dick in mothballs long enough in Russia, hadn't I?'

Occasionally he'd manage to borrow a car from the Armistice Commission. 'Some of our brave boys are suffering in the heat, sir – they need the cooler air of the mountains,' he'd say – and with a day's ration of petrol, he and Irma would drive into the mountains to fill their nostrils with the fresh scent of Aleppo pine. Curving up the dusty steep roads, they passed hard-faced men tending flocks of hardy sheep, women dressed in black, toothless, with faces like parchment, urging dwarf donkeys on unknown errands. There the two of them would picnic on the cropped grass, with the sound of the clear mountain streams bubbling and chuckling in the background, and then, when they were filled and half-drunk with the heavy red Algerian wine, they would make love as if they were alone in the world.

In Russia, the German Army fought its way to Stalingrad, then found itself trapped. In Germany, a thousand bombers knocked Cologne to pieces – the first of the German cities to be wiped off the face of the earth. In France, the Canadians landed at Dieppe and were cut to pieces by concentrated German fire, and in Britain they prepared to strike back massively on land for the first time since the Dunkirk débâcle.

Otto, enjoying his time out of the war, knew nothing of this. Nor did he care what was happening far away in war-torn Europe, as 1942 gave way to 1943. 'All I was concerned with,' he recalled many years later, 'was keeping a good thing going. For all I cared, I could still be living in Algiers in 1983! Of course, we had to be a bit careful, in case those shits from the Commission tumbled to our little game. But the frog doctors, Valmy and Hurwitz, were great. Every time the Commission descended on us to check whether our wounded were fit to go back to Russia and have their daft blond turnips blown off for "Folk, Fatherland and Führer", they'd have them lying in bed with a forty-degree fever, puking their guts out and looking like death warmed up – blokes who'd been out on the tiles the night before, sticking their salamis in the local frog gash and Eyetie nurses left, right and centre! It was the injections the two bone-menders gave 'em which did it. Natch, the Commission arseholes were suspicious, but a good Eyetie dinner followed by a roll in the hay with one of our girls in the nurses' quarters usually made 'em see the error of their ways. Those days in Algiers, it was all "you scratch my back, I'll scratch yours".

'It was a tremendous time. But nothing lasts in this world. As old Goethe – you know, the old fart who used to write books in Germany – said, "*Alles ist ein Werden und ein Vergehen*"[1]. Things change, I suppose you could say. You know – the joke about the old guy who used to feed the pigeons in the park? First you feed 'em and then they shit on you – from a great height!

'It was the same with the Count. By this time it was

[1] Roughly: 'All things develop and disappear'.

starting to get hot in Algiers, ready for the summer. As usual, he'd gone completely apeshit: he'd started dressing himself up in a bed-sheet with a face-cloth wrapped round his head, bare feet and sandals – the whole bit, even eating that *cous-cous* muck the wogs nosh, with his right hand, of course, and grabbing for the sheep's eye when they did a roast, as if the ugly shitting thing was a great delicacy. He'd even give the old belching appreciation thing afterwards. The whole works! But I could see it wasn't enough. He began to start sitting and staring into nothingness with that crappy "what-does-it-all-matter?" look in his glassy orbs. One word from me that summer of 1943 and he was off, talking ten to the dozen, crying stinking fish and moaning that life had become all "so purposeless" – there was no adventure any more.

'*Grosse Kacke!* Didn't he just get up my nose when he started that shitting lark!

' "*Adventure!*" I'd explode (the heat was pretty terrific by then and Irma was a bit much for me in that climate anyway). "I shit on adventure! People get killed dead in adventures! Here we are, eating the kind of nosh we ain't seen in the Reich since '39, with all the nookie a man could want, sunshine instead of that cold in Russia which'd freeze anybody's outside plumbing up – *and you want adventure!*"

' "Ah, but my dear boy," he'd say sadly, rolling his eyes, which looked like peeled hard-boiled eggs, "that's pure materialism, hedonistic materialism. There's more to life than the pleasures of the stomach and the bed."

' "Yes," I'd sneer at him, "like getting a slug through your skull. Some adventure!"

'He'd get me so riled, with his silly schoolboy's enthusiasm that I'd bugger off down to the kasbah and watch the belly dancers fling their fat stomachs at me and revolve their tits in different directions until I was shittingly well dizzy with the sight. But it didn't help in the end, natch. It never does. If I hadn't been such a dum-dum that summer I should have tumbled to what was going on – the way old Doctor Whore's-Joke used to bugger off at night on mysterious errands, for instance. Yeah, he was an Ikey, all right, and he had every reason to work for the Tommies or the Amis, or whoever he spied for. Another thing I ought to have noticed was how that warm brother Lemercier went cold on his running-mate old Mortello, and how the number of Chantiers de la Jeunesse got fewer and fewer each Sunday morning in the Grande Place. But of course, I was up to my glassy orbs in tits. Eyetie, Frog, Wog tits – that's all I could see that summer, and it was my downfall, believe you me. *Big tits – they've always been my downfall!* The great days were coming to a swift end, and all I did was to play with nipples . . .'

FOUR

The task force presented a brave sight, the Colonel thought, as he stared out over the side of the *SS Ancon*. Thirty transports and cargo vessels lay spread out over the miles of glittering green sea, bearing the assault infantry, with a screen of forty or fifty destroyers milling about like polo ponies. In the distance could be seen the reassuring grey bulk of the battlewagons – the *USN Texas*, *New York* and the newly commissioned *Massachusetts*.

Just to the Colonel's immediate rear the tannoy crackled, and in company with the hundreds of nervous young men in new khaki who crowded the rails to catch their first glimpse of Africa, Colonel 'Roaring Red Rory' Mulligan turned to listen to the announcement.

'Soldiers,' the voice of Major Gardner rasped metallically, 'we are now on our way to force a landing on the coast of North-West Africa. We are to be congratulated on being chosen as the units of the United States Army to take part in this great American effort.'

Somebody farted contemptuously and a young GI standing next to him gave a rousing Bronx cheer. Roaring Red Rory grinned, in no way offended. The boys of the good 'ole AEF had done just the same in 1917 when they'd docked at Le Havre and old 'Black Jack' Pershing had given them the same kind of crap.

'Our mission is threefold,' Gardner continued, unaware of the cynical reception his bold words had received on the deck of the troopship. 'First, to capture a beachhead; second, to capture the city of Casablanca; third, to move against the German, wherever he may be, and destroy him.

'We may be opposed by a limited number of Germans. It is not known whether the French African Army will contest our landing . . . During the first days and nights after you get ashore, you must work unceasingly, regardless of sleep, regardless of food. A pint of sweat will save a gallon of blood.'

Roaring Red Rory tensed. For twenty years now he had been in publicity – ever since he had been separated from the good 'ole Rainbow Div. He knew that so far the 'Old Man's' message was pedestrian. It had no oomph. It wasn't the kind of stuff that would make some young doughboy go in and chance his arm.

'The eyes of the world will be on you . . . God is with you . . . We will surely win . . .' Gardner's voice continued to drone out the old clichés; then suddenly, he cleared his throat over the tannoy, as if embarrassed; 'and . . . er . . . remember this. Keep your – er – goddam pieces dry, men, 'cause a wet rifle is as much use to you as a pecker is to the Pope!'

Gardner ended his message in a rush, to the wild cries and catcalls of the delighted young GIs. '—signed G. S. Patton, Jr, Major General, United States Army Commanding.'

The big Colonel grinned and winked across at the lean grey shape of the *USN Augusta*, which bore his master, General 'Blood an' Guts' Patton. 'Attaboy, Georgie!' he chortled, delight written across his broad red Irish drinker's face. 'That's the stuff to give the troops.' Then he forgot his idol, as the guns of the great ships swung round menacingly towards the dimly-perceived shore.

The softening-up bombardment would commence soon, and already the first GIs were beginning to swing themselves over the sides onto the disembarkation nets, while the *Ancon*'s engines slowed down to a soft throb. Hastily he donned his helmet, now newly adorned with his new slogan, 'AAO-O', stencilled on it in bold white letters – '*Anything, anytime, anywhere, bar nothing*'. 'All right, you

Joes,' he called to the waiting camera crew from the US Army Signal Corps. 'Let's haul arse! The big war's scheduled to kick off in ten minutes.'

Hurriedly the men began to swing themselves onto the nets, laden with equipment and cameras, trying to roll with the wallowing troopship as they fought their way down to the waiting Higgins boat. Roaring Red Rory grinned down at the bunch of Hollywood cream-puffs now masquerading as soldiers. One little shell from a Frog *soixante-quinze* of the type he remembered so well from the old war, and the whole gang of them would cream their skivvies there and then! Cupping his hands around his big humorous mouth he cried, 'Move it, you lot of canteen commandoes. Open yer legs. Nothing'll fall out—'

But the rest of his exhortation was drowned as the great 15-inch guns of the *USN Texas* thundered into violent, ear-splitting life. The great invasion of North Africa had commenced.

As the Higgins boat ground to a halt, the naval yeoman had to yell to make himself heard above the roar of the guns and the angry snap-and-crackle of the small arms fight which was taking place to their right. 'All right this is as far as we go! This is the terminal!'

'Christ on a crutch,' one of the Hollywood cream-puffs cried in horror. 'We're still in the middle of the fucking ocean! And I can't swim!'

'Now's the time to learn, Corporal,' Roaring Red Rory said, gripping his carbine more firmly in his big freckled hands. 'Because the Frog in that bunker over there—' he indicated the squat concrete pillbox some hundred and fifty yards away '—is drawing a bead right on you.'

That did the trick. The GI was over the side of the boat in a flash, dropping right into chest-deep water.

Roaring Red Rory dropped lazily over the side after them, carbine held cross-wise at chest-height, and began to slog his way to the beach, his nostrils suddenly filled with a stench – an amalgam of cordite, burning wood and smouldering flesh – which he hadn't smelled since Château-Thierry in 1918. Ploughing his way through the soft sand, which clung to his boots, he ignored a slow French machine-gun chattering somewhere in the smoke off to the right, and joined his ashen-faced, trembling camera crew, who were staring at the body of a dead GI, slumped face-downwards in the wet sand, helmet tilted to one side, hands still gripping his Garand, for all the world as if he had just lain down and gone to sleep.

'He's dead!' one of them said in a tiny awed voice.

'Knock it off!' the big Colonel said without rancour, and in a routine sort of movement, bent down and pressed the dead soldier's eyelids closed. 'Before this war is over, son, you'll have a bellyful of stiffs, believe you me.'

He straightened up, while the camera crew stared at him as if he had just arrived from Mars, and took a deep and enjoyable breath of air while he scanned the beach, with its discarded weapons, its half-dozen dead GIs and French soldiers. 'Great,' he said, 'just great!'

To their left front a group of infantrymen and combat engineers were getting into position to assault a pillbox set back from the beach on a small dune. The big Colonel flashed a look at his watch. The Old Man wasn't scheduled to land for another hour yet; they still had time.

'Okay, you guys, get the lead out. Let's get some prelim. action shots. They'll go fine with the ones of the General hitting the beach.' Seeing the camera crew hesitate, he added cheerfully, 'Come on, boys, this'll get you on the front cover of *Life*. You'll all be another Frank Capra.'

The promise seemed to work wonders. The photographers started to stream after him as he strode imperiously towards the assault group, a big grin on his red Irish face. 'Goddam Hollywood fairies,' he muttered to himself. 'They'd do anything to get their names in lights!'

As he arrived, the men were crouching carefully in the

sand, leaning on their weapons, while the combat engineers busied themselves with their demolition charges. The man at the BAR fired a burst of white tracer at the pillbox, aiming his slugs with considerable skill around the firing slit so as to deter the unseen defenders from grouping themselves round the small cannon that peered out of it.

'Attaboy!' Roaring Red Rory cried enthusiastically. 'That'll give them something to think about!'

The two officers in charge turned and stiffened to attention when they saw the silver bird on the big man's collar.

'Colonel Mulligan,' he introduced himself, and grinned. 'No military courtesy on a battlefield, boys. We left that chickenshit stuff back home in the ZI[1]. Now what's the drill?'

'I'll take it with explosive,' the engineer said quickly.

'No, you won't!' the infantry officer snapped angrily. Red Rory could see from his big class ring that he was a typical West Point hotshot. 'My doughs can do it on their own—'

Just at that moment, the West Pointer stopped short. An undersized Frenchman, wearing carpet slippers with a cigarette glued to his bottom lip, had appeared hesitantly at the entrance to the pillbox, waving a dirty white flag.

'Oh, shit!' the engineer officer cursed. 'The yellow bastards! All that training back in Georgia, all this darned explosive to get rid of, and look what they've gone and done. It ain't fair.'

'Give 'em a burst from the BAR,' the big Colonel suggested hastily, fearing for his action shots. 'That should do the trick.'

The BAR man tucked his weapon into his right shoulder and squeezed the trigger. Tracer cut the dawn sky viciously and tiny spurts of sand erupted around the carpet-slippered feet of the little Frenchman. For a moment longer he continued to wave his flag, cigarette still glued to his

[1] Zone of the Interior, i.e. the States.

bottom lip; then his nerve broke. Dropping the flag, he scampered back into the pillbox, slamming the steel door after him.

'Great!' Roaring Red Rory chortled happily. 'Okay, you cameramen, you get ready, while these gentlemen from the infantry and engineers give you a little demonstration of their various skills.'

Thus it was that as General George Patton Junior's boat started to edge its way through the littered breakers towards the North African shore and he prepared to make his dramatic landing on the scene of his first battlefield since 1918, the pillbox exploded in a great flash of violet light, the blast wave rocking the Higgins boat back and forth.

Undaunted, the tall, lean, grey-haired General stood up, putting on what he called his 'War Face Number Four', a hard-chinned, eagle-eyed scowl. 'Just look at that!' he cried in his surprisingly high-pitched squeak to his suddenly pale-faced staff. 'Could anything be more magnificent? You know, compared to war, all other forms of human endeavour shrink to insignificance.' Patton's voice shook with emotion as he girded up his twin, ivory-handled pistols prior to stepping over the side of the rocking boat. '*God, how I love it!*'

Behind him, one-eyed Colonel Gay blew a shrill blast on his whistle and beat his boss into the surf, carbine held across his chest. Immediately from the accompanying boats, military policemen, each one of them well over six foot, dropped into the water, flanking the General, tommy-guns held at the ready, eyes searching their front suspiciously.

Perfectly groomed in his London-tailored uniform, big cigar stuck jauntily out of the side of his thin face, his lacquered helmet with its two outsized silver stars gleaming in the first rays of the sun, Patton began to wade through the surf for the shore, while to his front Colonel Mulligan's camera-crew filmed the historic moment. As he reached the beach, apparently overwhelmed by a sudden emotion, he fell to his knees and clasped his hands together in prayer.

His staff hesitated and looked red-faced. But not Colonel Mulligan. 'Hot shit!' he gasped. 'The Old Man's praying! Great . . . great . . . Get it in the can, for Chrissake, you yo-yo! It'll wow 'em back in the 'ole ZI!'

'. . . If it be my lot to die, let me do so with courage and honour,' Patton intoned solemnly against the *thump-thump* of the ships' guns and the crackle of machine-gun fire further inland, '. . . and in a manner which will bring the greatest harm to the enemy. Please, oh Lord, protect and guide those I shall leave behind, and give us the victory, Lord . . .'

For what seemed like an age he remained kneeling there in silence while the cameras whirled and Roaring Red Rory danced up and down with delight; then he rose, carefully dusted the sand from his elegant riding breeches, winked at Mulligan and said, with a grin, 'Got it in the can, Red?'

'You betcha, General!'

'That's my boy!'

Majestically, followed by his entourage and guarded by the grim-faced, suspicious MPs, he strode across the sand to the gleaming waiting scout-car. A moment later he was gone, standing upright in the turret like some ancient Imperial conqueror, the vehicle's twin police sirens screaming.

General 'Blood an' Guts' Patton had arrived in North Africa.

FIVE

'*Pat-ton!*' the crowd cried hysterically. '*Vive le Général Patton!*'

Thousands of excited French voices took up the cry. '*Pat-ton . . . Vive le Général Patton!*'

Otto flashed a look at the Count. They were standing in the middle of a gay, excited throng of French men and women lining the Avenue de Bardo, waving French and American flags, cheering themselves hoarse, besides themselves with hysterical delight. The Count's face was as flushed and as excited as theirs. Otto let his shoulders slump. The Count was unbeatable. In a minute he'd be shouting, 'We're free! The Americans have liberated us!' Just like the Frogs had been doing all week.

Now the Spahis were cantering past on their white horses, sabres gleaming in the sun, cloaks billowing out after them. Now came the American outriders, eyes hidden by black goggles under brilliant white helmets, each man sitting ramrod-straight on his motorbike. In their midst came a khaki-clad band playing jazz, with the bandsmen doing strange little dance-steps.

The crowd gasped. So did Otto. He had never seen a military band like this in his life before. 'What – what do you make of that, Count?' he gasped. Just as he spoke, the drum-major did a sudden handstand, twirling his golden baton as he did so, while behind him the whole front rank of kettle-drummers stopped, did a sudden splits in perfect unison, jumped up again and marched on, not missing a single beat on their instruments.

'It's the New World, Otto,' the Count answered, completely unamazed by the strange performance. 'It's the spirit and energy of a young people.' He beamed as he watched the line of saxophonists suddenly break away from the band, swinging their gleaming silver instruments from side to side, and march up to a beaming old French matron in a strange hobbling step to give her a swift serenade. 'A fresh wind has commenced blowing into our jaded lives. After the long months of lying fallow, the fields are green again and are about to ripen—'

The rest of his words were drowned by a great roar that erupted from the delighted crowd as an enormous open touring car appeared with standing in its back, a tall lean soldier grasping the rail in front of him like a charioteer, his jaw jutting formidably against the webbing-strap of his highly polished helmet, saluting to left and right with an elegantly gloved hand.

'*Pat-ton!*' the throng cried again. '*Pat-ton!*' Everywhere they broke into spontaneous applause – even the Count, who was clapping as enthusiastically as the rest, his eyes gleaming with undisguised admiration.

'Is that *him*?' Otto asked, suddenly angry at the crowd and the Count. The man standing in the car looked no different from all the other generals he had ever seen – except perhaps that he seemed a bit more flamboyant than most.

'Yes, that's him,' another voice answered, in heavily accented German.

In spite of the throng pressed against him on all sides, Otto swung round.

An immensely tall American was standing there, a thatch of bright red hair peeping out of the side of his jauntily tilted overseas cap, a good-humoured, even amused smile on his red drinker's face. Next to him, dwarfed by the big soldier, stood a beaming Docteur Hurwitz, nicknamed 'Whores' Joke' by his former SS charges.

'May I introduce you all,' said Hurwitz, his German

sounding more Yiddish than ever. 'Colonel Mulligan, meet two colleagues of the resistance.'

'*Resistance!*' Otto gasped as the Count turned round to stare up at the gigantic red-haired American officer.

'Monsieur le Comte von der Weide,' Hurwitz said, indicating the surprised Count.

Roaring Red Rory thrust out a hand like a steam shovel. 'Put it there, your Honour!' he boomed in English. 'Give me five. Sorry – my German just gave out.' He pumped the Count's hand enthusiastically. 'One thing about you aristocrats – you're at home all over the world!' He winked with mock solemnity. 'I guess that's why you guys make the best agents.'

Otto felt a sudden ominous thrill of fear and gave a shiver.

'A louse run over your liver, Monsieur Stahl?' Hurwitz asked a little anxiously.

'Something like that,' Otto said non-committally, wondering if he had heard correctly. Had the big red-faced Ami said '*agent*'?

'You must look after yourself. This time of the year the climate here in Algiers is particularly bad.' Hurwitz raised his voice. 'And this, *mon cher ami*, is Monsieur Otto Stahl, of whom I have spoken to you already. This is the man who effectively sabotaged the schemes of those boches of the Armistice Commission to send the SS resisters back to the front.'

'SS resisters—' Otto began, but he didn't get far. Colonel Mulligan's great paw engulfed his and he yelped with pain as he felt the full impact of the American's bone-crushing grip.

'I've heard a lot of good things about you, Mr Stahl,' Roaring Red Rory said enthusiastically. 'The Doc here and Doctor Mortello back at the hospital told me how you smuggled those brave SS fellows, who risked death in the fight against fascism, to safety here. Pity you aren't in the good 'ole US Army yourself – there'd be a medal in it for

you. But not to worry. That'll be taken care of in due
course. General Patton'll see to that.' He indicated the
erect, elegant figure now disappearing from sight and
beamed down at Otto. As if he had known the pair of them
for the last hundred years, Colonel Mulligan placed his
arms around the shoulders of the two running-mates and
began gently to shepherd them through the departing
crowd towards the big olive-drab Packard waiting for
them, with Doctor Hurwitz trotting behind like an anxious
hen.

Twice Otto opened his mouth to ask questions, but both
times the big American silenced his queries with a smile
and a wink. 'Security, you know, fellers. Can't be too
careful!'

Finally they were ensconced in the plush back seat of
the big car. 'Okay, Rastus,' Mulligan said to the coloured
driver. 'Take her away. Back to General Patton's HQ.'

'*General Patton's HQ?*' the two friends gulped in startled
unison. But by then the car had pulled smoothly away,
with the driver honking furiously at a crowd of barefoot
Arab boys who had clustered around it, begging for money
and crying, 'You jig-jig sister, *Americain?* . . . You jig-jig
momma? . . . You jig-jig *me?*'

'You can tell those youngsters like us,' Mulligan said
with a good-natured chuckle, as the Arab boys fell behind,
making obscene gestures with their middle fingers and
lifting their gowns to exhibit their naked loins. 'It does ya
heart good to see their gratitude. Say, Monsieur Stahl,
what does "jig-jig" mean?'

For a moment Otto was tempted to explain, but then he
remembered that word 'agent' and said angrily, 'You said
General Patton's HQ, Colonel – why?'

Mulligan countered with a question of his own. 'Does
the name Sicily mean anything to you, Monsieur Stahl?'
His eyes narrowed significantly.

'No,' Otto answered bluntly, while the Count stared at
the big American with unfeigned admiration. 'Should it?'

'Sure,' Mulligan answered easily. 'Because that's where 'ole Blood an' Guts is going next. He needs a couple of smart operators like you guys to tell him what's waiting for him over there.' The Colonel winked at a suddenly pale-faced Otto. 'We know all about you guys' record with the Abwehr. Why, if that little birdie told me right, you fellers have even worked with the Limey Secret Service as well!'

'A new adventure!' the Count chortled happily, clapping his plump, well-manicured hands together in sheer delight like an over-excited child. 'At last, a new adventure!'

For his part, Otto simply groaned and let his shoulders slump in defeat. The good times in Algiers were over for them. Instinctively he knew it was back to the shooting war for them. There was no escaping their fate. Wishing he was dead, he closed his eyes to block out the crazy, cheering world outside and let the Packard speed him to his new date with destiny . . .

OTTO STAHL 1: OTTO'S PHONEY WAR

Leo Kessler

On the night Hitler's Panzers roared into Poland, Otto was working undercover with the sergeant's wife.

Crook, conman, casanova, blue-eyed Otto Stahl is equally at home with an eager fraulein or a batch of black market coffee. A natural coward with a genius for saving his own skin, Otto dodges the German draft – only to be catapulted into frontline action against the Dutch tank regiments.

Decorated by Hitler, stripped by Himmler, seduced by a nymphomaniac Countess, and relentlessly pursued by SS headhunters, Otto bluffs his way from bedroom to battlefield and back.

The bawdy, bloody and hilarious adventure of one man's war which tells the inside story of the Third Reich as it has never been told before.

Futura Publications
Fiction/War
0 7088 2027 1

OTTO STAHL 2: OTTO'S BLITZKRIEG!

Leo Kessler

Continuing the bawdy, bloody and hilarious adventures of the greatest conman and casanova in the German army.

Only Otto Stahl could turn capture in a mobile brothel into becoming a hero of the Third Reich.

Safely tucked away in a mobile field brothel in the north of France, Otto thought he had the rest of the war sewn up. Until the night commandos raided the coast and whisked Otto off to a POW camp in England. But, resourceful as ever, Otto cons his way out and home to Germany – to a hero's welcome and the unwelcome honour of a special assignment from the Fuhrer himself.

Futura Publications
Fiction/War
0 7088 2173 1

All Futura Books are available at your bookshop or newsagent, or can be ordered from the following address:
Futura Books, Cash Sales Department,
P.O. Box 11, Falmouth, Cornwall.

Please send cheque or postal order (no currency), and allow 45p for postage and packing for the first book plus 20p for the second book and 14p for each additional book ordered up to a maximum charge of £1.63 in U.K.

Customers in Eire and B.F.P.O. please allow 45p for the first book, 20p for the second book plus 14p per copy for the next 7 books, thereafter 8p per book.

Overseas customers please allow 75p for postage and packing for the first book and 21p per copy for each additional book.